Rose

*A
Harlequin
Romance*

Rose

OTHER
Harlequin Romances
by ELEANOR FARNES

Many of these titles are available at your local bookseller,
or through the Harlequin Reader Service.

For a free catalogue listing all available Harlequin Romances,
send your name and address to:

HARLEQUIN READER SERVICE,
M.P.O. Box 707, Niagara Falls, N.Y. 14302
Canadian address: Stratford, Ontario, Canada.

or use order coupon at back of book.

THE
SPLENDID LEGACY

by

ELEANOR FARNES

HARLEQUIN BOOKS   TORONTO
WINNIPEG

Original hard cover edition published in 1973
by Mills & Boon Limited.

© Eleanor Farnes 1973

SBN 373-01765-0

Harlequin edition published March 1974

Printed in Canada

CHAPTER I

Cristina was leaving her desk to go and take dictation from her employer when the telephone rang and she turned back to answer it.

'Cristina?'

'Oh, Vernon, hallo. Can't stop now, darling, I have to go and take dictation.'

'I only wanted to make sure about the weekend. You are coming?'

'I certainly am. Lovely to get out of London.'

'I'll call for you around seven and we'll eat at home. How have you been?'

'Stunned, mainly.'

'*Stunned?* Why stunned?'

'By some unexpected news, but I'll have to tell you about it later. Can't stop now, I have to go.'

'What a cliffhanger! All right, Cristie, until seven, then.'

Cristina continued on her way, knowing that Vernon would be as surprised as she had been. When he arrived at her minute apartment promptly at seven that evening she was ready, her sheepskin jacket lying on the couch beside her suitcase and a fringed leather bag.

They flew into each other's arms, for Vernon had been out of town for five days. Their kiss went on for some time. 'Ah,' said Vernon at last, 'I've been waiting for that.' He kissed her again, lightly, swiftly, this time. 'Now what about this news? What's happened? Ernie? or have you won the pools?'

'Something rather like it, but I'll tell you on the way. It's quite a long story, and I don't want to miss dinner. I'd rather eat your mother's food than my own.'

'I'd better not say—So would I,' he commented.

'No, or I'll never cook for you again.'

'On our way, then,' he said, but before she could pick up her belongings, he had taken her into his arms again and she had lifted her face for his kiss, holding him as closely as he was holding her. 'I missed you,' he said as he gently released her.

'I missed you, too.'

They gathered up Cristina's things and went out to the car.

'Now,' said Vernon, as they drove out of the side road into the mainstream of traffic, 'what was this unexpected news?'

'Well, you know I've never gone in for much family history; mainly because there was nothing to report. You know my father died when I was four and my mother married again when I was ten. She married an American and went to live in the States, but they didn't want *me*, which seemed a perfectly heartless thing to me. I was shipped off to my grandmother, her mother, and I lived with her for nearly ten years. Grandmother was really a bit of a tartar, she believed in discipline for young people. I was at a day school and life wasn't too bad; she let me have friends at home, and visit them in the holidays, and even put herself out to take me for dreary seaside holidays which neither of us enjoyed much.

'Anyway, when I left school, I wanted to get a job, but Grandmother had quite decided she wanted a companion. She had a cook, and a daily, but she wanted somebody to drive her about, so she bought a car and I had driving lessons and became her chauffeur; and changed her library books and washed the precious porcelain and helped in the garden. A comfortable life, but a damned dull one . . .'

'I can imagine. Did you never rebel?'

'I brought up the matter several times about getting a job. Once I was even so rash as to suggest going to London and sharing a flat; but that really brought her wrath tumbling about my ears. She said: After all she had done for me! After she had changed her whole way of life for my benefit! God knew my mother was selfish, abandoning her own child and planting her on Grandmother, and now I was turning out to be from the same mould. Completely ungrateful! Had I got anything to complain about?

'I hadn't, of course. I was living on the fat of the land, but it wasn't what I wanted. Anyway, I gave in. I saw myself getting old in her service. But then Miss Usher turned up. I'm not boring you, am I?'

'No, I'll let you know when boredom sets in. Who was Miss Usher?'

'Miss Usher was a very clever lady. She was then between forty and fifty. Very slender means, overanxious about getting married. She bought a small cottage in our village, made it look very pretty in a chintzy sort of way, and began to join everything. Now my grandmother used to run everything at one time, and she still had a finger in a few pies; and in no time at all, Miss Usher was buttering her up and flattering her and running about for her; and eventually was invited home and was *most* impressed by all Gran's worldly possessions. *I* believe she made her campaign right then and went to work on it. Sure you're not bored?'

'Get on with it, love, I want to hear what the Machiavellian Miss Usher was up to.'

'She wanted my job, of course. She didn't know that I wanted to lose it. It was amusing, in a heartless way, to watch her manoeuvres; to see her ingratiating herself with Gran and squeezing me out. I remember one afternoon I wanted to play in a tennis tournament but Gran wanted to drive to some fête miles away. So of course Miss Usher was *delighted* to drive her, and Gran decided she liked Usher's driving much better than mine—it was slower and more sedate, I suppose—so from then on, Usher drove more and more and I less and less.

'I didn't really mind. In the end, things went my way. Grandmother consented to my coming to London with Barbie Mills—remember Barbie? her mother and mine were once great friends. We roomed together for two years. Well, Miss Usher moved in to take my place, and she and Grandmother got on famously.'

'And what is the unexpected bit?' asked Vernon.

'I'm coming to that, but you have to wait a moment. Miss Usher effected quite a transformation in my grandmother. They began to travel all over Europe and my grandmother fell in love with France; and the upshot of that was that she bought a house in France that calls itself a chateau, and went to live there permanently with Miss Usher, both of them perfectly contented. I got a postcard from time to time, and apart from those, Gran seemed to have forgotten my existence.

'But now Gran has died, and has been buried in France. And I think it very strange indeed that I wasn't told in time to go to her funeral. But— and this is what you've been waiting for, Vernon—

apart from a legacy to Miss Usher, Gran has left *me* the chateau and its contents and practically all she was possessed of.'

' When did you hear all this?'

' The day after you went north. Gran's solicitors asked me to go and see them; and I had all the news. There will, of course, be death duties, and there are various complications about French estate and English estate. The solicitors assure me they can take care of everything, but it seems that Gran was better off than I ever knew, and I'm no longer on the breadline, Vernon.'

' Congratulations, darling, but I *am* sorry about your grandmother.'

' I was, too. I was dreadfully weepy for a day or two, because she was almost all the family I had, and though she bullied me a lot, I'm sure she was fond of me in her way. Anyway, she left my mother some jewellery: nothing else because she said she didn't need it, and Gran disapproved of the way she had abandoned me. Everything else was for me!'

' Well, well, this is a surprise,' said Vernon. ' I had no idea you were an heiress, Cristie. What are you going to do about it all? What can you do with a chateau in France, for instance?'

' Sell it, I suppose. What do you think? I've been waiting for you to get back, to discuss it with you.'

' Aren't you dying to go over and see it? Is this Miss Usher still there?'

' Yes. And there's a family living in part of the place. Apparently, although Gran and Miss Usher both loved it, they *did* find it miles too big, so they had part for themselves, and rented part to this family. They, apparently, are quite ready to go on renting. Everybody, in fact, is waiting to know what the new owner—I—am going to do. And I still haven't got used to the news, and certainly haven't decided what I'm going to do.'

'Go over and see the chateau,' suggested Vernon.

'I don't suppose it's anything like a chateau, really; just a house with a few trimmings, I imagine. Would you come with me, Vernon?'

'If I can arrange some time off, certainly I would.'

'Oh, *do* try. You'd be *such* a support, and I should enjoy it if you were with me.'

'Bless you. I'll do what I can. I'll take part of my holiday. What about your job, Cristie?'

'I expect I'll give it up. It seems there'll be a lot to do, getting all Gran's affairs settled.'

There was a pause in the conversation and Cristina supposed that Vernon was considering her new circumstances; but when he spoke it was obvious that his thoughts had been in quite a different direction.

'Have you really got no family at all, Cristie, apart from your mother in the States?'

'I have an aunt and two cousins in New Zealand, but I don't know them and never hear from them. Otherwise, no one.'

'You poor dear. Haven't you often been very lonely?'

'Oh well . . . On the whole, not too bad. Times when I was a child, of course, and Gran was cross with me and I terribly resented my mother leaving me. Nothing, you know, that I couldn't get over.'

'Ah,' said Vernon, 'you're putting a brave face on it. When I think of my family, and the way everybody depends on everybody else, and the wholesale family discussions that take place, and the general rumpus, I think it must be pretty terrifying always to have to rely upon yourself.'

'That's why I find your family such bliss. They take me just as I am and make me feel at home.'

His was not the only family Cristina had known. Invitations from school friends had taken her into some homes with large families, but there had never been one with the warm ambience that surrounded the Walfords. There was real affection there, a lack of tension and undercurrents. When one stepped into the house, one felt the atmosphere of welcome. Vernon was very much a product of this, a whole person, well rounded, with the confidence in himself that the total security behind him had fostered. Cristina had been drawn to him on first meeting him, perhaps sensing this security and confidence. And he, for his part, had sensed in her the aloneness, the searching for an anchorage.

They discussed Cristina's change in fortune until they reached the house set in undulating countryside, still fortunately isolated, settled down into paddocks and gardens as it had been for nearly two hundred years. It was now dark, and the headlights of the car lit what seemed to be a tunnel of drive between the encroaching rhododendrons, before they opened out to a wide gravel circle surrounding an ancient cedar, and the car swept around this to stop at the porticoed front door.

Mrs. Walford, hearing the arrival of the car, came out of the drawing room to meet them.

'Lovely to see you both,' she said, kissing them in turn. 'I do hope you won't mind that we've already had dinner. The others were starving, but yours is all ready for you.'

'I know, we are a bit late,' said Vernon. 'I didn't leave the office until half-past six.'

'Well, go and take your things upstairs, and it will be ready for you.'

They went up the graceful curving staircase and parted at the top for their bedrooms. Cristina did not bother to change, but washed and saw to her make-up and went at once downstairs. 'Anything goes in this house,' Mrs Walford always said; and it was 'anything goes' this evening, for Anne was in a splendid Indian sari, and Flora was in trousers, with a soft mohair shawl, while Mrs Walford, as always, was trim in a tailored dress. A great log fire burned at one end of the drawing room, and Mr Walford was deep in an armchair at one side of it. He unfolded his long length to stand up and greet Cristina with a kiss on one cheek. He was scholarly, slender, grey-haired, with a wry humour.

Mrs Walford explained that Ralph was playing squash, and Noel would arrive about eleven at night. This completed the family. Three sons and two daughters; none, as yet, married. Vernon the eldest, Flora the youngest. Only Vernon and Noel were living away from home, and they came back for every weekend they could manage. This family atmosphere was what Cristina liked so much, but had never had.

Vernon and Cristina ate their meal in the dining room, and the food, as always, was good. The customary feeling of gratification stole over Cristina: a glow, a happiness, that she seemed to feel only in this particular house.

'Are you going to tell the family the great news?' asked Vernon.

'Why not? I'd like to hear their reactions,' replied Cristina.

So, when they went into the drawing room again and found Ralph added to the number, all of them in a wide circle round the fire, they drew up their chairs and Cristina told them what had happened, her news received with a ready interest. Anne asked, as Vernon had done:

'But what can you do with a chateau in France, Cristina?'

'Ask us to come and stay with you there,' said Flora promptly. 'Do you suppose it has stables and horses?'

Cristina laughed.

'Hardly! I imagine my grandmother's riding days, if ever she had any, were over long ago. And honestly, you mustn't build it up into a fantastic thing. I expect it's just a biggish house. The French will call anything a chateau.'

'Even so,' said Ralph, 'you have to do something with it.'

'Well, I suppose I shall sell it. But I've hardly had time to consider it yet. We've got as far, Vernon and I, as deciding we'll go over and have a look at it, as soon as he can get some time off.'

Cristina happened to look at Mrs Walford as she said this, almost as if she was seeking approval for this visit, and she intercepted a glance between husband and wife, fleeting, but also a glance of confirmation. It semed to say: 'We were right in thinking that things had gone a long way between these two.' And perhaps it was a pleasant factor that Cristina had come into a small fortune.

'It sounds very exciting,' said Flora. 'Where-abouts is it, Cristina?' And the discussion became very general, as Mr and Mrs Walford remembered driving through the exact area on one of their journeys abroad, and said what beautiful countryside it was, unspoiled too, and some of the villages still so peaceful and rural and out-of-the-way that they might be nineteenth-century still.

The party broke up and the family drifted off to the bedrooms. Vernon went into Cristina's room with her, his arm about her.

'I expect you've got all you need,' he said.

'Your mother would see to that. But she wouldn't approve of your being *here*, Vernon.'

'I know, but we have to have a moment to say good-night.'

She went into the circle of his arms, lifting her face for his kiss, and the good-night extended itself for moment after moment. 'It was a long week without you,' Vernon whispered between kisses. 'I don't want to leave you now.' And Cristina had to exert considerable will power to release herself at last and tell him that she must turn him out.

'Yes, I'm going. I expect the family will have us up early for riding.'

Cristina groaned, being fairly new to riding, and Vernon laughed at her, gave her a last hug, a last kiss, and left her alone to sleep. And Cristina was ready for breakfast with the family, for riding with them afterwards, on their own horses and some borrowed from the riding school. Only Mrs Walford stayed behind, to prepare lunch for them all. All the Walford children had been put on ponies at the earliest possible moment (Cristina said straight from their cradles) and were completely at home with them. All the Walfords were passionately attached to their horses and their dogs.

Cristina enjoyed her ride and returned with a good appetite for lunch, to find Noel added to the party and the family complete. In the afternoon,

Vernon carried her off for a country walk.

'You know, darling,' said Vernon, 'now, if we get married, people will say I'm marrying you for your money.'

'Let them,' said Cristina placidly. 'We know differently.'

'You notice that I said " if ",' he pointed out.

'Why? Have you changed your mind about us?' she asked him.

'I? Is it likely? You know that I want it more every day—want *you* more every day. But we have rather drifted into it, without anything definite. I don't want to take you for granted.'

'I don't think you're doing that. Make it definite, if that will make you happy.'

He stopped and took her into his arms.

'Would it make *you* happy? That's more important.'

'Yes, yes, it would. But I'm not really in any hurry, Vernon, are you?'

'I wouldn't want it to hang on until it lost its zip,' he said.

'Magic would be a better word,' Cristina reproached him.

'Has it got magic for you, darling?'

'Of course it has. One goes on, in a fairly level way, knowing all sorts of people; then suddenly one meets a new one and bang! everything becomes more exciting, more fun, more interesting.'

'And *I* did that for you?'

'You did.'

He held her more tightly and kissed her. A passing car did not disturb them. When they walked on again, he said:

'Then why aren't you in a hurry, Cristie?'

'Because this is such a nice phase in one's life.

15

I don't know if I want to start managing a house and meals and shopping and all that, yet. It's a kind of luxury getting to know each other. Having you and your nice family and these beautiful weekends, I'm very contented.'

And she was. When Vernon had driven her back to her apartment on Sunday evening, and left her to go to his own, she felt a satisfaction with life, a glow of content after her happy weekend, which she felt was almost too good to last.

Although she had made light of her loneliness to Vernon, saying that there was nothing she could not get over, there had been many times in her life when that loneliness had threatened to overcome her. Especially when her mother married and went to the States. It had seemed impossible that her mother could leave her behind with her grandmother, and in spite of the affectionate farewells and the presents that arrived from time to time during the first year or two, there were countless times when Cristina had cried herself to sleep in the big bedroom in the big house; and if Grandmother had suspected it, she did nothing about it. Even an only child had parents to love it and make a family for it; but she had only a rather stern grandmother.

The loneliness of London, too, for a newcomer with a bedsitter for home, could be terrifying at first. True, she had had Barbie, and Barbie had had her, and it had not been long before they made a circle of friends. But it was this background that made the Walfords so precious to her. The welcome and the warmth, the company and the many activities, the interweaving of all these personalities into the one thing she had never had—a happy family. When she looked into the future, she knew that she would like to be incorporated into this family herself.

They went in Vernon's comfortable car, crossing the Channel on a chill grey day with a high sea running, and Cristina relieved that the journey was no longer. In the warm car, speeding along the French roads, she soon revived; and by the time they arrived in Chartres she was in good spirits, had developed an appetite and was beginning to enjoy the trip.

They had a drink before dinner, and later enjoyed an excellent French meal in the restaurant of their hotel.

'Wonderful French cooking,' Cristina said. 'Even doing France on a shoestring, when my friends and I used the *routiers'* cafés, the food was always good. But this is delicious.'

'Why didn't your grandmother take you on those trips she took with the Usher lady? There would have been room for you too, wouldn't there?'

'She did write to me once that she had thought of it, but Miss Usher was sure I would find it dull being with two older people and would prefer holidays with my own "gang". She was terribly jealous, poor thing. But perhaps she was right at that, for we had fun although we were hard up.'

'At least your grandmother could have made you an allowance.'

'She did, and still does. But it's very small, because she thought it was my mother's duty to do that. But, to be honest, I think I hardly exist for my mother. She had two boys very quickly after she married her American, and a little girl some years after, and her full life doesn't leave any room for me.'

'Don't you feel bitter about that, Cristie?'

'Not in the least. Not now. I got over being bitter long ago. I live for the present and the future—our future, Vernon.'

After dinner they walked in Chartres, enjoying and admiring the floodlit beauty of the Cathedral, before deciding on an early night to ensure an early start next morning. They intended, by leaving early, to reach their destination the same evening.

This they did. Once they had left the main road, they found that the country became steadily more rural, the villages fewer and smaller, the occasional towns more provincial, the scenery more and more beautiful.

'My grandmother seems to have buried herself in the wilderness,' commented Cristina. 'I hope the house isn't too lonely, or I might not be able to sell it.'

'Privacy and quiet are things that many people want to buy nowadays,' Vernon said. 'And you don't know that it's lonely. There's a village there, isn't there?'

'Yes, I think so, but I really know very little about it.'

There was a village, one of the most attractive they had yet seen, in its somewhat primitive fashion. Most of the houses were of stone, many of them built at the foot of a cliff which seemed to tower over the village and hang over it; others built at what seemed precarious angles on ledges of the cliff itself. Beyond the houses on the opposite side of the street they glimpsed the falling away of the hill and the valley below. They asked the way of an old man in the village, who directed them to a road which climbed, zig-zagging, steeply and diagonally up the cliff itself. Cristina hung on with

both hands, nervous of the ascent. Vernon said:
'God, what a road! There must be some other
way of getting up here. How did your Miss Usher
manage it?'

'How did my grandmother stand it? Oh good,
it flattens out here a bit. We must be almost at
the top. And look, Vernon, is that the house? Can
it possibly be? No, surely not. Do stop a moment,
so that we can have a look.'

They had arrived at the top of the cliff road and
found themselves on a plateau across which the
white road ran straight to the gates of an old stone-
walled castle which looked immensely strong and
much more like a fortress than a house to live in.
Its square shape, pierced by a wide arched doorway
and windows of various sizes, was broken by a wide,
circular tower at one end, a somewhat squat tower
with the same air of immense strength. The pines
and other trees that surrounded it seemed wind-
blown, but as they drove nearer, they realised that
these trees provided the shelter for the gardens
inside. The car stopped outside the tall, closed
gates.

'Do you think that this can be it?' asked Vernon.

'I can only think my grandmother had gone
mad, if it is,' answered Cristina.

They looked about them. The dusk had rapidly
deepened, and it was now too dark to see very far,
but there was no sign of any other house about.

'We'd better make enquiries,' he said.

'I'm so glad I've got you with me, Vernon. Do
you suppose there's a gate-keeper somewhere?'

'We'll see.' They got out of the car and went
to the wide, tall gates. Vernon tried the big handle
and it turned smoothly. At his push the gates also
moved smoothly on their hinges, well oiled, well

looked after. He pushed them wide enough to allow the car to pass through, but before they got into the car again they stood and looked about them for a moment.

In the darkening evening, they saw that the wide flag-paved road led ahead of them to the arched doorway, widening out to form a large courtyard. To each side of where they stood, smooth lawns stretched away to shrubs and trees now being absorbed into the darkness.

'This is quite incredible,' said Cristina. 'I'm sure there must be some mistake. Besides, there are no lights. Nobody is living here.'

'It's all so well kept that I think somebody must be,' said Vernon. 'Let's drive up to the door and find out.'

They drove to the wide, regularly-paved courtyard, and went up to the impressive doorway. Vernon pulled on the iron handle at the side of it, and that too worked perfectly. The door was opened after a minute or two by a young, fresh-faced girl wearing trousers and a loose sweater, and looking eminently sensible and ordinary.

'Good evening,' said Vernon in his English-accented French. 'Can you tell me please if this is the Chateau de la Falaise?'

'*Oui, vraiment*,' said the girl.

'The house of Madame Marchant?'

'*Oui, oui*. Oh, but you wish the other part of the house . . .'

'Who is it, Marguerite?' A man had appeared at the back of the bare and lofty hall. He was a tall, dark shape in the shadows. Cristina could not see him well, but she thought his voice held a strange undertone of impatience or frustration. That was her first impression as Marguerite explained that the visitors wanted the house of Madame Marchant.

'Couldn't they see the signs inside the gate which quite plainly indicate where *we* are to be found and where Madame Marchant's entrance is?'

'Good evening,' Cristina said to the voice in the shadows, and she spoke in English, thinking that he was English too. 'I do apologise, but it's getting dark, and we didn't see the sign in our headlights.'

Marguerite explained in very broken English that many people had made the same mistake; and in her light, trilling voice she directed them to go by the round tower to another entrance where they would find Mademoiselle Usher.

'P'raps you not know Madame Marchant *est morte*?' she asked, trying to subdue the gaiety in her voice to a sadder note.

'Marguerite,' said the man's voice, 'that will do now.'

'I do know,' Cristina said. 'She was my grandmother.'

At that, the man came out of the shadows, stepping through that bare hall to the magnificent doorway. And they saw that he was tall and slim, elegantly dressed, dark of hair and eyes and quite unsmiling.

'I'm sorry,' he said. 'Of course I didn't know who you were. Please come in.' They stepped into the bare place with its vaulted ceiling. 'I offer you my condolences on your grandmother's death. I admired her very much. I was her tenant, you understand, and I began to know her very well.'

'Thank you,' said Cristina. 'Perhaps you will be kind enough to show us where we can find Miss Usher.'

'May I first introduce myself?' he asked. 'I am

21

Alastair Buchanan, and I've been renting a part of the chateau from your grandmother for nearly a year.'

'I'm Cristina Howard, and this is my friend Vernon Walford.'

There were general acknowledgements and then Cristina, explaining that they had been driving all day, once again mentioned Miss Usher.

'The quickest way is through this hall, which is part of the shell of the old chateau. But you'll want to take your car round. Past the tower, it's the first entrance. You should find it lighted.'

They thanked him and he held the door for them.

'I'm sorry you've come on such a sorrowful mission,' he said. 'Au revoir.'

Cristina and Vernon got into their car and drove slowly round by the tower, when the light of her grandmother's entrance became immediately visible, shining out across the paving to the darkness of the trees.

'So that's the tenant,' commented Vernon. 'Melancholy-looking chap. But thawed out a bit when he knew who you were.'

'He wants to go on renting the place, so perhaps that made him sweet. He talked about the shell of the old castle, so perhaps it isn't as vast as it first appeared.'

The car stopped at a smaller version of the first doorway, and the door opened as they were getting out of the car. Miss Usher came out to greet them and to help them with their bags.

'Cristina,' she said, and in the French fashion kissed her on both cheeks. As they had certainly never been on kissing terms, this surprised Cristina. 'I hope you had a good trip down. You must be tired. Here, let me take that.'

'Miss Usher, this is Vernon Walford,' Cristina said, and the two shook hands. 'You did get my message that he would be coming with me?'

'Yes, my dear. It was nice for you to have a companion. Everything is ready for you both. Come along in. The car will be all right there.'

They went into a moderately sized hall, comfortably furnished with deep sofas, and warmly lighted.

'I'll take you to your rooms first, and then I'm sure you would like dinner. It's all ready. *Coq au vin,* one of dear Mrs Marchant's favourite dishes.' She led the way upstairs, on to a corridor from which opened several doors. 'I've put *you,* Cristina, in one of the tower rooms—I thought you would find it interesting. Mr Walford is opposite, at the end. Come down as soon as you're ready.'

Cristina went into her tower room, listening for Miss Usher's step retreating along the corridor and descending the stairs. Then she popped her head out of the door, to find that Vernon had opened his door, too.

'Give me a knock when you're ready, Vernon.'

'O.K., I'll do that.'

The circular room would have been uncomfortably large but for the fact that a bathroom and dressing room had been carved from it so cunningly as not to spoil its shape but to render it more oval than circular. A large window had been set into the thick wall, but at the moment was covered by lined silk curtains. The furnishings bordered on the luxurious, mainly cream and blue; the carpet blue, a cream fur quilt completely covering the bed. Cristina thought her grandmother had certainly gone to town.

She decided there was no time for a bath and the

appeal of the *coq au vin* was considerable, so she washed her hands and face, changed her slacks and shirt for a dress, and was applying fresh make-up when Vernon tapped at her door.

'Come in,' she called. 'I won't be a moment, Vernon.'

'My, my, you are splendid,' he said. 'What luxury!'

'Isn't yours splendid, too?'

'Much simpler. The bachelor's room, but nice. Your Miss Usher is much more pleasant than I expected, Cristie.'

'Too pleasant, methinks. Butter wouldn't melt. I suspect such pleasantness. Miss Usher has a little explaining to do; but I'm not going to press her, I want to see the lie of the land first.'

Vernon crossed to her side.

'Do you think I might kiss you *before* you put that lipstick on? Then you won't have to repair it afterwards.'

She went gladly into his arms, lifting her face to his. It was Vernon who at last slowly released her.

'Vernon, I am glad to have you here to support me,' she said.

'And I'm glad to be here. Now come along, love, put on that lipstick and let's go down to our *coq au vin*.'

The dining room, to which Miss Usher led them from the hall, was also of a comfortable size, and although beautifully furnished, had no special distinguishing features. As Miss Usher brought in a handsome soup tureen and asked them to be seated, one at her left, the other at her right, Cristina commented on this.

'Is this a new part of the chateau, Miss Usher? It doesn't bear much relation to that awe-inspiring exterior.'

'Completely new, my dear. The place was quite a ruin when your grandmother took such a fancy to it. The previous owner had restored the façade, and did it so well that he ran out of money and was glad to find a buyer. But inside the shell there were the run-down living quarters where the Buchanans now live, and the splendid round tower. Your grandmother and I both derived a great deal of pleasure from having this new part built, incorporating the tower rooms.'

The soup was delicious. The *coq au vin* which followed was equally good. If Miss Usher had fed her grandmother like this, Cristina thought it might have been a satisfactory relationship after all. Vernon declared the wine to be excellent.

'Oh, I think we were both developing quite a palate,' said Miss Usher modestly. 'Yes, about this chateau. It was quite obvious, once this new part was built, that we weren't going to need the whole place; but we restored it nevertheless, with the idea of letting it to some nice people. I'm not so sure that the Buchanans are nice people—but there, that's another story. They came so well recommended that your grandmother let them have it, and *she* certainly seemed to get on well enough with them.' Did Cristina imagine it, or had some bitterness crept into Miss Usher's voice as she spoke about the Buchanans?

After dinner, Miss Usher took them into the *salon* saying she would bring coffee almost immediately. Vernon and Cristina were left to admire the room by themselves. It was the lowest floor of the round tower and half as high again as the other rooms, with a vaulted ceiling, the stonework filled in with narrow brick. The walls seemed to be almost half window and Cristina imagined the view would be marvellous by day. A stone fireplace was now filled with green plants, but the room was so warm that Cristina realised central heating had been installed. Here again, the furnishing was luxurious. 'My grandmother must have spent a fortune on this place,' Cristina said quietly to Vernon. 'I can't help thinking she must have been egged on by Miss Usher.'

'But you must admit it's a marvellous and fantastic place, Cristie. I'm keen to see it by daylight.'

'Yes, it is lovely. And interesting.'

'And it's *yours*, darling.'

'Heavens, yes, I still find that incredible. It's *mine*.'

The door had opened as Cristina spoke that last sentence and Miss Usher appeared with the coffee tray. As Vernon went to take the tray from her, Cristina glanced at her, wondering if she had heard what was being said, and surprised a look of such malevolence on her face that she was left in no doubt. Miss Usher *had* heard Cristina saying: 'It's mine,' and did not like it at all. Cristina, who had been prepared to be on her guard when dealing with Miss Usher, was even more prepared for it now.

Miss Usher seated herself behind the coffee tray in silence.

'This is a charming room, Miss Usher,' said Vernon pleasantly. 'Part of the old castle, of course. Was there much of the old building you were able to retain?'

'Very little. The tower, of course, and the hall, which was intact. The outside wall and a few rather crumbling flights of steps. Most of the rest was so unsafe it had to go. Black or white,

26

Cristina?'

' Black, please.'

The three of them sipped their coffee in silence. Cristina thought she must take the bull by the horns, and said:

'Miss Usher, I thought it very strange indeed that I wasn't informed of my grandmother's death in time to come to her funeral. How did that happen?'

'Oh dear, oh dear, I've been in a terrible state about that, Cristina. I really do apologise. I couldn't think what to do for the best; and it did seem to me that your grandmother had cut you off, so to speak. . . . Of course, we know *now*, since the reading of the will, that she intended no such thing, but I didn't know it then. I'm dreadfully afraid that I was guilty of saying that there was no family. I see now that was very wrong of me, but you know, in the stress of the moment . . .'

Her voice tailed away. Cristina hardened her heart.

' But my mother! Gran's own daughter! Quite apart from myself, how do you think *she* would feel?'

' Your mother,' Miss Usher said coldly, ' has consistently neglected both of you for the last fourteen years. Why should *she* be remembered now? What can she do now that her mother is dead, if she did nothing for her when she was living? I have no qualms whatever about your mother.'

' Or me, apparently.'

' I've already apologised for that. I have, after all, devoted six years of my life to Mrs Marchant. I say, without any false modesty, that I made those years happy ones for her. She was continuously interested and enjoying life. So that, when she

27

died, it seemed the most natural thing in the world for me to take charge of affairs as I had done for six years. The regulations are different here in France: there was a great deal to be seen to on the spot. So I saw to it. As I say, I see now that it was wrong. But I did it for the best—in a time of great grief for me—I was very fond indeed of your grandmother.'

Tears appeared in Miss Usher's eyes. She produced a small handkerchief to cope with them, and rose hastily to her feet.

'You must excuse me,' she said tremblingly. 'I'm afraid I'm still upset. . . . I lost a dear friend. . . . I will say good-night to you now and we can talk in the morning . . .'

Vernon hurried to the door to open it for her.

'Good-night, Miss Usher,' he said kindly. 'Try not to be upset.' And when she had gone through, he closed the door behind her.

'Poor old girl,' he said to Cristina. 'She's taken this hard.'

Cristina gave him a straight and level look.

'I don't trust her an inch,' she said.

CHAPTER II

The morning was cool, bright and sunny. Cristina drew back the curtains of her oval room to find that she had a wide-ranging view over beautiful country-side. The tall trees they had noticed last night impeded this view to her right. Before her and to the left, the cliff top hid most of the village from sight, and beyond the village there was a panorama of valleys and hills, steep bluffs crowned with trees, a wide twisting river. Within the sheltering trees, the garden was pleasant and very French, laid out in formal beds with box edging, the paths converging on the centre where there was a marble fountain. Turning to her left again, immediately below, was the wide path leading to the gates, and the lawns on each side of it. Everything seemed to be very well kept.

She was a little puzzled. She knew her grandmother to be comfortably off, but not on this scale. Perhaps it was the Buchanans who kept the whole place in such fine fettle. She felt that there was still a great deal she needed to know, and hoped that Miss Usher was not going to dissolve into tears whenever a serious subject was broached. True, she might be really grieving. Six years of living with somebody were likely to form a strong tie. But she had been very much in the wrong, and Cristina thought she knew it very well.

A tap at her door was followed by Vernon's appearance.

' Ah, you're up,' he said approvingly.

' And all ready. Come and admire my view.'

He crossed to her side, putting an arm round her

29

shoulders to turn her towards him, kissing her long and tenderly. 'This is the view I like,' he said. 'Dark gold hair and gold-brown eyes.'

'But I want you to look at the view outside.'

'Yes, that's really something. I could retire very happily into a place like this. But only if I make a fortune.'

'What's yours like?'

'The garden and tall trees. No real view, but very pretty. *You* are the important person here, darling.'

'It's a strange feeling. Let's go down to breakfast. I do hope there'll be *croissants*.'

They went out of the door, and Miss Usher was in the corridor. She looked astonished to see them coming out together, but recovered quickly and said only:

'Ah, there you are. I was coming to see if you would like French breakfast or the English kind. I do have bacon and eggs.'

'Have you *croissants*, though?'

'Actually, yes. The baker sends his van up specially to the chateau, for the Buchanans and ourselves.'

'Then French breakfast, please, Miss Usher.'

'And Mr Walford?'

'That will be fine for me, too.'

'It's no trouble to cook you something.'

'Another day,' he said, smiling at her, and she smiled back at him. Cristina thought Miss Usher was probably surprised to find this sympathetic attitude in Vernon, knowing that he had come along to watch Cristina's interests.

Miss Usher did not join them for breakfast. She had had hers—she was an early riser, she admitted.

'If you would like to have a discussion with me,

Cristina, I shall be available whenever you wish. And Mr Buchanan would like to see you too. Naturally, he wishes to know where he stands, and what arrangements he might have to make. So if you'll let us know . . . I must apologise for being so silly last night.'

' I'm sorry we upset you. And I'm free for you, or Mr Buchanan, whenever it suits you both.'

It was arranged that Cristina should see Mr Buchanan at eleven in the morning and that she and Miss Usher would have a talk after lunch.

' You will come with me, Vernon, to see this man?' she asked, when they were alone.

' If you want me to, Cristie, but these are all your private affairs.'

' I haven't anything private from you, Vernon.'

' Bless you. Of course I'll come, then.'

So they went to find Mr Buchanan together. They could see, from inside that heavy, impressive wall, that it was indeed but a shell. Only the round tower and the hall projected from it, encroaching on to smooth lawns; and on the farther side of the hall, was the house where the Buchanans lived: a house very typically French of the nineteenth century, and strange to find within these old walls. It had an air of being completely cut off.

The door was opened to them by Marguerite of the dancing eyes, who informed them that Monsieur awaited them, and led them to a warm, cosy and unexpectedly light room arranged as a study.

Alastair Buchanan rose to greet them. Very tall, very dark, still unsmiling, still, in his casual clothes, elegantly dressed.

' This is kind of you, Miss Howard, to see me so soon.' He indicated chairs by the window and joined them there. ' May I ask, is Mr Walford your man of business?'

'Oh no,' Cristina said candidly. 'Vernon is my friend, but you may speak quite frankly, for I have nothing private from Vernon.'

'I see. Very well, then. You will understand, I'm sure, that my main interest just now is what is going to happen to this house. I realise that you, Miss Howard, as the heir, may not yet have decided what to do, but I thought if I explained my position, it would give you something to go on.'

'Please do,' said Cristina. 'The news of my grandmother's death and my inheritance were both a great surprise to me, and I haven't yet decided anything. I came over simply to see the chateau for myself and find out what was going on.'

'What was going on?' he asked in surprise, his dark eyes fixed on her face.

'I thought it strange that I wasn't told in time to come to the funeral.'

'Ah. That, of course, I can't comment on.' He plainly was not going to intrude on what was not his business. He glanced at Vernon, who was listening and watching, but most of the time his dark eyes rested on Cristina. 'I understand that you would want to see for yourself. And I realise that you have no plans for the moment. But for myself, there are several possibilities. I would like to go on renting this house. If, however, you decided to sell it, and would sell the two houses separately, I should like the first opportunity to buy; but you may wish to sell the whole property. I thought I would make my position clear so that you can take it into consideration.'

'Yes, I will. I have to think everything over and consult my solicitors; but I should think it would have to be sold. What use have I for a place like this, beautiful as it is?'

' And would you consider selling as two properties?'

' I can't decide on anything at the moment, Mr Buchanan, but I will remember what you have said.'

He told them the rent he was paying for the house which caused Cristina to open her eyes wide. It seemed an enormous amount. He said the place suited him very well, and seemed anxious to stay there.

Cristina was about to say they must be going when he offered them a drink, and she sank back in her chair to wait for it. He pressed a bell and after a few minutes it was answered by a middle-aged woman in a large white apron.

' Where is Marguerite?' he asked in French.

' She is out of doors with the children.'

' Ah, then would you, Marthe, please ask Mrs Buchanan to come and join us in a drink.'

The woman went away, and as Alastair Buchanan joined them, glass in hand, Cristina said to make conversation:

' Is Marguerite your daughter, Mr Buchanan?'

' No, no. She's nursemaid to the children.'

' I didn't realise you have a family,' she said.

' I haven't,' he said sombrely; and as Cristina was thinking that the children must then belong to his wife from a previous marriage, he went on: 'It's apparent that Miss Usher has not told you anything about us.'

' Not a word,' said Cristina, ' but please don't think I'm being inquisitive. It doesn't matter.'

' Miss Usher doesn't approve of us,' he said ironically. ' And as your grandmother seemed to appreciate my friendship, Miss Usher approved even less. I felt sure she would have said a great deal about us.'

Marthe reappeared at that moment to say that Mrs Buchanan begged to be excused. She had a bad headache and was lying down.

'She's a little shy of strangers,' Alastair said. 'It's rather too remote here. She should go out more in society, but she doesn't have a taste for it. Now, perhaps I should tell you how things are run here. I made myself responsible for the garden, which I would be happy to go on doing. Mrs Marchant liked the old French design, so it was kept. I made myself responsible too for the general tidiness of the exterior; the lawns, gates, pavements and so on. I have a young man to help me.'

'We both thought how beautifully everything was kept.'

'Thank you. Let me get you another drink.'

They both refused, and Cristina rose to leave.

'I'll keep you informed, Mr Buchanan, of what happens,' she said.

'I would appreciate that,' he said, his dark eyes looking into hers.

'And I hope your wife is soon better.'

'Mrs Buchanan is not my wife,' he said. 'It's a very common misunderstanding. She is my late brother's wife, my sister-in-law.'

'I'm sorry,' exclaimed Cristina.

'There's nothing to be sorry about,' he said. 'For she will, very soon, be my wife.' He saw the puzzlement on Cristina's face and added: 'It's not really a complicated situation, although some people try to make it so.' He opened the door for them. 'I hope to see you again,' he said. He nodded his head at Vernon in goodbye, and showed them out of the house politely enough. They

34

walked back to the other house, in silence for a few moments; but, safely out of earshot, Cristina said:

'Well, well, what do you make of that?'

'Saturnine sort of chap,' said Vernon.

'Oh, did you think so? Last night you thought he was melancholy, now saturnine.'

'What did *you* think of him?'

'I think he *looks* distinguished. I don't know what I think about him otherwise. It's a strange sort of situation, don't you think?'

'A bit odd, yes. Perhaps that's why Miss Usher disapproves, if she's a bit strait-laced herself.'

'Though one might consider him noble and generous to make a home for the wife and children of his dead brother.'

'Isn't it carrying nobility a bit far to marry her too?'

'Ah well, it's not our problem,' said Cristina, 'but I wonder why she didn't come to have a drink with us? I sense a mystery.'

'Perhaps she did simply have a headache,' said Vernon, smiling, 'and *you*, Cristie, are coming under the influence of old castle walls and a romantic atmosphere.'

They laughed comfortably together.

'I could have asked to see the house, Vernon, seeing that it's part of the property.'

'That will come,' he said calmly. 'Plenty of time. We have three complete days here; in that time you have to see the lawyers and sign their forms, and decide about the immediate future. Miss Usher, for instance.'

'What about her?'

'It seems to me, simply as an outsider, an observer, that she had done a good job here. No doubt, even if your grandmother had the ideas, a lot of the donkey work fell to Miss Usher. Probably she enjoyed it—I imagine she did—but she did it all the same. And she's a splendid cook. And the house is very well cared for, immaculate, in fact.'

'She's getting very well paid for it, Vernon.'

'Probably no more than she's worth. But I was thinking that she might be a good person to leave in charge here until you've decided what to do. She knows the ropes, after all.'

'It's strange to find you so much in sympathy with her.'

'I'm simply going by what I see. There are two sides to every question, Cristie.'

'Well, don't forget *my* side. You don't know how diplomatically and with what guile she got me out of my grandmother's house. As it happened, I wanted to go; but suppose I hadn't wanted to go, she would have got me out just the same.'

'You can't be sure of that. I expect your grandmother knew what was going on. She knew you wanted your freedom.'

Cristina shook her head.

'You just didn't see the way Miss Usher went about it. She looks harmless and pleasant, but she's wily and clever.'

'Clever enough to make your grandmother's life very happy and interesting in her last years.'

'Why, Vernon, you're on *her* side!'

'Nonsense, darling, I'm for ever and ever on your side; but I'm astonished, to tell you the truth, to come up against this implacable bit of your character. You do have a down on the poor lady.'

'Well, she's very clever if she's succeeding in putting a wedge between us.'

'Cristie, Cristie, you goose! Who's putting a

wedge between us?' He stopped and caught her into his arms, regardless of who might be watching them from either of the two houses, and kissed her passionately, until, at last, she gasped for breath. ' Now,' he said, gently releasing her, ' have a bit of sense, girl. Besides, if anybody succeeds in driving a wedge between us, I won't be able to marry your fortune. Remember that.'

' What a good thing you fell in love with me before we knew anything about it,' she teased him. ' You'd never have dared to afterwards.'

They walked to a spot where the massive wall finally crumbled away into a belt of trees, walked round it to the outside, and over the lawns towards the main path and the main gates.

' This man Buchanan has certainly made a fine job of all this,' commented Vernon. ' I wonder what he does, if he does anything. For a living, I mean. What *can* he do, cut off in this remote place?'

' Private means?' suggested Cristina.

' Odd sort of life, all the same. It would drive me mad.'

' Because you, darling, are so gregarious. Your lovely big family, with so much going on, your job, meeting so many people. Besides, you're young.'

' He's hardly old. He can't be all that much older than I am.'

' He *seems* older, anyway.'

' That's the melancholy I was talking of. And why are we talking of him, when we could be talking about us, and this astonishing change in your fortunes. Just look at it, Cristie. Stand here and look. Isn't that magnificent?'

They stood and admired the mellow colouring of the stone, the impressive strength of the round

37

tower. 'Yes, but it's comforting to know that it's only a shell, and manageable inside. Much easier to sell.' Vernon opened the gate and they went through, and strolled across the plateau to the edge of the cliff. The stone houses of the village lay beneath them, with a backcloth of hill and valley.

'Lovely country for riding,' said Vernon. 'I wonder if we could nobble a couple of horses anywhere?'

'Perhaps Miss Usher could tell us. Ask her at lunchtime.'

Vernon, who was never quite happy without a horse at hand, did so.

'Why, yes, Mr Buchanan has two horses right here, and ponies for the children. There are very good stables here. I suppose you could approach him. I daresay he would allow you to ride.'

After lunch, Miss Usher brought the coffee to the tower room and suggested that she was ready to discuss anything that Cristina had in mind. She seemed to expect Vernon to leave them, but Cristina said once more that she had nothing private from Vernon.

'Well, there's something I would like to tell you at the outset,' said Miss Usher. 'Mrs Marchant gave me several presents during the last year or two. Some jewellery and various other little treasures. I have no way of *proving* that they were given to me, but I should be very sorry to have to part with them.'

'What were they, exactly?' asked Cristina.

'I have them here.' Miss Usher produced a box into which she had gathered these treasures. There was a beautiful sapphire and diamond ring, a smaller ring of three diamonds, a straight pin of small rubies and pearls. There was also a small gold box, a Chinese figure in jade, and some old-fashioned tortoiseshell combs for the hair, one ornamented with a line of brilliants.

'This is quite a valuable treasure chest,' said Cristina.

'I'm afraid I don't know the value of these things. This little pin was the first present, for my birthday about three years ago. The sapphire and diamond ring was given me when this house was completed.'

Cristina looked at Vernon, and Vernon was watching her intently, and she knew intuitively that he was wondering if this 'implacable' side of Cristina's character was about to emerge again. She looked at Miss Usher.

'If these things were given to you, Miss Usher,' she said, and was there the slightest stress on that first word that implied doubt? 'they belong to you and we wouldn't wish to deprive you of them.' But she felt sure that her grandmother had never given them away. She knew her too well. Yes, she might give presents, the pearl and ruby pin, the combs; but she would not part from her much-loved jade figure, or the small gold box she kept her hairpins in—and certainly not the sapphire and diamond ring she was so fond of.

They went on to discuss other matters until it was time for Vernon and Cristina to drive away from the village to the nearest town to see the notary. They were silent as the car negotiated the rough and steep downward bends, but when they picked up speed along the country roads, Cristina was still quiet and thoughtful.

'What's the matter, Cristie?'

'The jewellery,' she said.

'What worries you about it?'

' I don't believe Gran ever gave it to her.'

' Why should you doubt her word? She was very straightforward in telling us about it.'

' She had to do that. But my grandmother had a very strong sense of *family* values. I can understand she might give the ruby pin or the fancy combs; but I happen to know she was passionately attached to the jade figure and the gold box, and I don't believe for one moment she would give them away. But what can I do about it? It's her word against mine—and mine is only suspicion.'

' Even if she helped herself, Cristie, and there isn't a scrap of evidence to show that she did, what does it all amount to? A thousand pounds? Perhaps she felt that she had earned that.'

' It would be much more than that, and people have been jailed for much less. And when you say " helped herself ", you mean *stole*. Well, I think she did. She had plenty of time to go through Gran's things before I knew what was happening. And how do we knew that what she showed us was all?'

' Darling, don't be so bitter. It doesn't suit you to be so suspicious, and perhaps every word was the truth.'

' Well, I don't like her and I don't trust her. She's been on to a good thing for the last six years.'

' So what do you intend to do?'

' I won't keep her on.'

' That's obviously the only thing to do if you dislike her so much.'

Cristina knew that he thought her unreasonable. Vernon did not know how cleverly Miss Usher had ingratiated herself with Mrs Marchant in the first place. They sat in a somewhat uncongenial silence, which in itself was so unusual and so unwelcome that at last Cristina burst out:

'And now you're sitting there thinking me so hard-hearted and inflexible, without really knowing the true facts of the case . . .'

'Cristie, I know you're the kindest-hearted girl in the world, but you do seem to have a little blind spot about Usher. Here's a poor soul, probably alone in the world . . .'

'Well, you don't know *that*, for a start. And I don't want us to quarrel about her. Let's change the subject.' But the subject, although temporarily ignored, was a small sore spot between them.

They finished their business with the notary. Everything was quite straightforward, the French lawyer was in touch with the London solicitors, and Mademoiselle could be assured that there would be no undue delays. They went for a drive, and gradually their good humour returned, their temporary disagreement about Miss Usher forgotten. But it could not be completely forgotten, for the moment they stepped into the house, there she was in the hallway waiting for them, smiling, saying:

'Ah, I thought I heard the car. I hope everything went well with the notary. I'm sure you're ready for a little aperitif, and the tray is ready in the *salon*.'

'That would be very welcome,' said Vernon, but Cristina went upstairs saying she would be down in five minutes. She wondered how she would tackle the unpleasant task of getting rid of Miss Usher, and walked to the window, looking out thoughtfully. Immediately, she saw Alastair Buchanan down in the garden, applying a dressing of some sort to the paths. He was casual in slacks and a roll-neck sweater, and in this casual wear still, to Cristina's eyes, managed to look distinguished.

Dark hair, heavy dark eyebrows, a brown skin. And still the slightly sombre expression. As she watched, two young boys came running from a doorway in the wall, chasing each other, hopping over the low hedges, leaping round Alastair when they reached him. About eight and six, two slender, leggy boys with dark hair, and even from this distance Cristina could hear their high-pitched chatter. Then Marguerite appeared with a small girl of about three years old, a charmer with her dark curls and her hop, skip and jump along the pathway. Alastair swung her up in his arms, and Cristina saw only his back as the whole party began to return to the house. Perhaps Marguerite and the children had been sent to fetch him. They all went through the pointed archway in the wall and disappeared from her sight. Cristina hastily ran downstairs to join Vernon and Miss Usher in the *salon*.

It was very comfortable and pleasant there. Tall lamps were already lit to send a golden glow about the room, leaving the lofty ceiling in shadow. Vernon was deep in an armchair with a glass in his hand, listening to Miss Usher telling some story of her travels with Mrs Marchant, and Cristina did not feel like disturbing the peace for the moment. It was easier and more congenial to take an armchair near Vernon's and wait for Miss Usher to bring her a drink. 'My favourite poison is Pernod,' Miss Usher said, bringing Cristina her home-made and delicious cheese puffs. Everything was harmony on the surface, and Cristina decided not to ruffle that harmony just now.

'I suppose, Cristina, you have no definite plans for the house yet?' asked Miss Usher.

'No. It's rather soon. I'm still taken aback by

events. But the only course I can see before me is to sell it.'

'You haven't considered keeping it?'

'Whatever for? What could I do with it?'

'You could live in it. Or you could let it and derive a good income from it. Especially with the income from the other house.'

'But there would be a lot of maintenance, surely?' said Vernon.

'Not for a long time, because everything has been recently done. The façade well restored, this house newly built and the other restored and decorated. And Mr Buchanan maintains the gardens.'

'It would be super to come here for holidays, Vernon, wouldn't it?' asked Cristina. 'Your family would love it. Riding and everything. But of course, that's just a pipe dream and not very practical. I guess it will have to go.'

'If I can be of any help to you,' Miss Usher said, 'if, for instance, you do sell, I could be here to show people round.' And suddenly Cristina's distrust returned.

'Too early to make arrangements,' she said. 'When I marry, I suppose I shall live near London, for Vernon's work . . .'

'Oh, congratulations, both of you, I didn't realise that you were engaged.'

'We aren't,' said Cristina. 'We'll get married when we feel like it.'

'You young people! What different notions you have about life these days. Now please excuse me, I'm going to watch over my pots and pans. I hope you have a good appetite for dinner.'

She went out and Vernon stretched out a hand to Cristina. At once she abandoned her chair, dropped a cushion on the floor at his feet and sank down on it. He leaned forward and kissed her, and she put up a hand to bring his head still closer to her, her fingers in his hair, lost to the world. At last, he took her hand away, kissing her fingers, and then leaned back in his chair again, keeping her hand in his.

'After dinner,' he said, 'I'll start checking on the inventory. That isn't a job you particularly want, is it, Cristie?'

'I don't want it at all. Is it necessary, really?'

'The lawyer seemed to think it should be done, but you needn't concern yourself. If you trust me, that is.'

'If there's one person in the world I do trust, it's you,' she said. So that after dinner, with sympathetic explanations to Miss Usher of why he had to check the inventory, Vernon started on the work, and Cristina said she would like a little fresh air, and went out of the arched front door into a world made magic by the black and silver and grey of moonlight.

The night was very still and the sky cloudless, so that the nearly full moon shone with brilliance over the lawns and courtyards, and the intricate pattern of the wide entrance gates was duplicated in clear outline on the wide paved path. The tall trees threw dark shadows, but the fountain with its small trickle of water keeping the basin full to overflowing shone resplendent in white marble, occasional drops of water sparkling like diamonds. There was such peace overlying the whole garden, the whole countryside, that Cristina herself was suddenly at peace, taking deep breaths of the pure, cool night air.

She walked between box hedges into the shadows of trees, and suddenly started and exclaimed in alarm, as a shadow emerged from all the other shadows.

'It's all right, please don't be frightened,' said the voice of Alastair Buchanan. 'I saw you coming and would have left you to your walk, but there's a runnel of water here which you might not see and might step into. It's very dark just here.'

'Thank you,' she said. She could see it now, a quite wide runnel in a stone trench. 'I could easily have fallen over it,' she admitted.

'It's perfectly safe, but people don't usually make the acquaintance of the garden at night time. Now you know it's there, all is well.'

'Isn't it a wonderful night?' she said. 'So soft and clear and even warm.'

'If you come along here a little farther, you can see the village by moonlight. It's really quite attractive. Give me your hand and you can step across.'

She could have stepped across unaided, but the moon and the shadows did make queer effects, so she gave him her hand and stepped over the runnel of water.

She gave him her hand. Such simple words, such a simple action; an action that people were making all day long, shaking hands with each other, offering and taking things with casual hand touchings. But when this man took her hand in his long, strong, cool fingers, there was something in the touch almost electric. Cristina thought it was ridiculous to imagine that something passed between them; yet there it was, a current, a spark, a joining together that seemed to make it difficult to let go, to separate again. There was a perceptible pause, when both of them stood still, waiting for what would come next. Then he took a stride forward and she followed him, in a dream, until they stood at the spot he had mentioned, gazing down through a wide gap in the trees at the village that seemed to sleep in the tranquil moonlight.

'Yes, it's lovely,' she said at last, breaking the bemused silence. 'I must go back now.'

'Let me guide you through the shadows,' he said, and went before her, holding a tree branch out of her way. At the runnel of water, he extended his hand. Her instinct was to say: 'I can manage thank you,' but her curiosity was paramount, the curiosity to discover if that first effect had been but imagination. She took his hand, and stepped over, and he did not immediately release her. And the strange contact was still there, almost a flowing together like two drops of mercury, so that it needed an effort of will to remove her fingers from his. They came to the marble fountain.

'There are no more dangers ahead of you,' he said.

'Then I'll say good-night, Mr Buchanan.'

'May I ask how long you are staying?'

'Only two whole days more, I'm afraid. Vernon has to get back to work. And that reminds me. Miss Usher tells us you have riding horses, and we were wondering if you would be so very kind as to let us ride tomorrow morning.'

'With pleasure, but one of them is a mettlesome creature and needs strong handling.'

'Vernon is an expert. He has ridden all his life. But I'm not much good, I hope your second horse isn't mettlesome.'

'No, you can trust Countess, she's good and docile. When do you want to ride? I'll have them saddled and ready for you.'

'Nine-thirty? Or is that too early?'

'That's fine. Good-night, Miss Howard.' He extended his hand again in the French fashion, and again she took it, before turning her back on him and making for the round tower; and she was not sure, but she thought she heard him whisper intently to himself: 'My God!' She would not look round. Did it mean, she wondered, that he had experienced the same extraordinary feeling of some sort of communion as she had? How odd, she thought, how very odd; and longed to turn back to see if he was watching her, but pride would not allow it. Before she went into the house, she stood in silence for a few moments in the tranquil night, trying to regain tranquillity herself. Not with complete success.

Vernon had had enough of the inventory for one evening. As soon as Cristina returned, he stopped work to join her in the tower room. Miss Usher was not there.

'I met Mr Buchanan in the garden,' she said at once, trying to make it sound the most ordinary affair in the world. 'So I asked about the riding, and it's all fixed for tomorrow at nine-thirty. Suit you?'

'Fine.'

'He has a very mettlesome horse for you, but a quiet one for me, thank goodness.'

'Fine,' said Vernon again. 'As long as he likes me, I like a bit of spirit.'

'You're referring to the horse, of course.'

'Naturally. In fact, I didn't notice so much spirit in Mr Buchanan. I hope his horse has more. Well, darling, up betimes tomorrow and a good breakfast and a wonderful gallop.'

He put his arms round her, and with a sudden twinge of guilt, a twinge of conscience perhaps, she threw her arms round his neck and kissed him with so much passion that he was delighted, and drew her closer still; and it was only the reappearance of Miss Usher that at last caused them to part.

CHAPTER III

When Alastair Buchanan handed the horses over to Vernon and Cristina next morning, he said:

'When you come back, I'll show you the stables and the tack room, and I'm sure, Miss Howard, you would like to see the house and exactly what your property consists of.'

'Yes, I should. Thank you,' said Cristina. She was mounted on Countess, who satisfyingly did seem to be the good, docile creature that Alastair had described. Vernon, before he mounted Firebrand, talked to him quietly, stroked and patted him, while Alastair watched.

'We called him Firebrand because as a foal it was almost impossible to contain him and his lively temperament. He hasn't outgrown it, the name suits him still.'

'You've had him a long time, then?'

'Yes, we brought them both out from England, and ponies for the boys later. Well, you look as if you won't have too much trouble, Mr Walford,' and Alastair stood back to watch them set off, Firebrand tending to dance nervously, Countess placid enough even for Cristina's inexperience.

At the end of the ride, Vernon admitted that Firebrand had been quite a handful, and that Alastair Buchanan must be pretty good to tame this handsome but certainly mettlesome horse.

Alastair came out to meet them. He handed the horses over to a young man to care for, and proceeded to show them the stalls, the tack room, the fodder, pointing out that some of these old French buildings, farms, stables and barns, were more picturesque than many of the houses. Their tour concluded, he said:

'Now do come and see the house. But after your ride, you would probably like to have a drink first.'

They walked across the cobbles of the stableyard and over the lawns that led to the house, and into a sitting room by means of french windows. Drinks were already set out on a side table, but there was nobody in the room, although Marguerite put her head round the edge of the door a few moments later, informing them that Madame was coming downstairs immediately.

Cristina was very curious to see this Mrs Buchanan. She knew a few facts about her already: that she had been married to Alastair Buchanan's brother, that she had three children, who, from some distance, had seemed to Cristina to be charming, spirited and beautiful. Presumably her husband had died, and perhaps without leaving her too well provided for since she was now being cared for by her brother-in-law. Cristina tried to remember if such a family arrangement was above suspicion, but she knew of none like it. But Alastair had said, when Cristina had presumed that she was his wife: 'There's every probability that she soon will be my wife,' so perhaps they were engaged to be married. With a son who appeared to be about eight years old, she would probably be about thirty herself.

Cristina had admitted that she would prefer a glass of dry white wine to any other drink, and now Marguerite had brought it in and Alastair was drawing the cork.

'There you are,' he said, proffering the glass which was already beginning to mist over from the chill of the wine. 'A Montrachet Lassigny just at its best—a drink fit for a princess.' He bowed slightly. 'We were to drink it for luncheon,' he added, so that she immediately refrained from sipping it.

'Now you've made me feel guilty,' she said.

'Please don't. It's not the only bottle. It's a pleasure to give you pleasure.'

The door opened and a slim young woman appeared, dressed in a grey trouser suit of superb cut, her dark hair pulled smoothly back into a knot at the back of her neck, small pearls at her ears, diamonds sparkling from her fingers. Her face was oval-shaped with small, regular features, and her skin was faultlessly olive; but it was her dark eyes, surrounded by eyelashes that Cristina could hardly believe were natural ones, that put a stamp upon her beauty. She looked much too young to be the mother of those spirited boys.

Alastair performed the introductions, and this beautiful creature was indeed Mrs Angus Buchanan. She was very shy, Cristina thought, almost nervous. She had a glass of the wine Cristina was drinking, accepted it from Alastair, and sat down in the group, but performed none of the duties of hostess. She left everything to Alastair, the drinks, passing the small dishes of appetizers, offering cigarettes— which neither Vernon nor Cristina smoked. She left the conversation to him too, smiling at her visitors from time to time, but apparently having nothing to say.

'Sylvana is very much hoping that we will be able to stay here,' Alastair told them. 'She likes it here and feels at home here.' He had almost said 'she feels safe here' and hardly knew why he changed it at the last moment. 'If we can go on renting, we shall be very pleased; and if that isn't possible, we would think about buying.'

'Well, of course, I will consider you and Mrs Buchanan, but there are so many other things to consider too that I must have time to think everything over.'

'Naturally. We don't want to hurry you. If it's a question of rent, I would be willing to agree to a slight increase: one knows how expenses are rising all the time.'

'No, no, it isn't a question of rent,' Cristina said hastily, for she thought he was already paying an exorbitant one.

She was waiting, with some interest, for Sylvana Buchanan to say something of her own accord. Sylvana, she thought. An Italian name, surely? Why, of course, she looked Italian. Everything about her was Italian. She had not said enough to betray a foreign accent, but Cristina thought her speech might sound Italian too. But, in fact, by the time they rose to go and look over the house, she had added nothing to the conversation, did not accompany them but left the guided tour to Alastair, and saw them go with a charming smile.

The house was pleasant and spacious, beautifully decorated and comfortably furnished, but with nothing particularly historic about it until they came to the corridor that connected it with the ancient hall of the chateau, which was a kind of no-man's-land between the two houses and which nobody used although the boys had been known to ride their bicycles there on wet days.

Mrs Buchanan had disappeared when they finished their tour and it was Alastair who saw them out.

'If you would like to ride again tomorrow, you're very welcome,' he said, and they accepted his offer with pleasure.

It was almost lunch time and they made their way back to the other house, taking the path that led round the ancient hall and then crossing the lawn to their doorway.

'What a beauty!' commented Vernon, of Sylvana Buchanan.

'Absolutely,' agreed Cristina.

'Beautiful but dumb?'

'Well, she had nothing to say for herself. Just shy, perhaps?'

'Abnormally shy, if it's only shyness. And I think *she*'s the one who wants to stay here.'

'I suppose the remoteness suits her. Could those gorgeous eyelashes possibly be her own?' Vernon laughed. 'Oh yes, you're thinking it's sour grapes, I know . . .'

'Nothing of the sort. For me, I much prefer my golden English rose.'

'Ugh, that makes me sound so insipid.'

He laughed again.

'It's true. All the freshness and colour and stunning beauty of an English rose. Honestly, darling, I so much love your candour and fun and freedom and intelligence that other men can have the sultry beauties and the dumb ones.'

'Still, supposing I didn't sell my chateau, they'd be quite attractive neighbours.'

'Cristie, you aren't thinking of keeping it?'

'No, no, it was just an idea that slipped in. One of the ideas to think about, Vernon.'

It was an idea, however, that persisted in slipping in, more by way of a pleasant day-dream than in any practical sense. Cristina had not accustomed herself to the idea of being a property owner and a well-to-do young woman, but to dream of herself living here was a pleasant form of relaxation. No Miss Usher, of course. Perhaps some other, nicer person to do the housework and cooking. Herself and Vernon, riding together, exploring the French countryside together, returning to her grand-mother's charming house, small enough to be manageable, high on its plateau, open to the fresh airs of heaven but sheltered from its roughest winds by its belt of trees and its ancient castle wall.

Practical considerations brought her down to earth. Vernon lived and worked in England, his family lived and worked there too, and it was Cristina's home place. Perhaps her apartment was hardly ' home ', but England was, and London was, and the Walfords' house; and indeed the whole web of places and people that made up her life. What would be wonderful, she thought, would be for Vernon to provide the two of them with a home near London, and for the chateau to be waiting for them for holidays and as many visits as they could manage to make.

She said something of this to Vernon, who re-garded her somewhat ruefully, shaking his head at her.

' I'm not sure that we should be able to live in such fine style as that, Cristie. I'm doing pretty well, but that needs real money.'

' Apparently I do have some real money. You could run the house in England, couldn't you? because if we got married and. . . .'

' What do you mean: *if* we got married?' he interrupted her.

' Figure of speech, darling. *When* we get married. Well, if you could do that, I could run the French one—especially with the help of that exorbitant rent the Buchanans pay.'

'It isn't exorbitant when you consider the place they're getting; the castle atmosphere, the house itself, stables and so on. But of course it's a great help. But you wait, Cristie, my love, until you get away from here and are back in England. Things will settle down into their right proportion. No need to do anything in a hurry. We can come over again.'

We can come over again. There was suddenly a reassurance in his words. Yes, she wanted to come again. She knew it wholly, completely. She wanted the house to be here to welcome her. She liked it. She was already fond of it. She wanted to come soon.

'Let's come for summer holidays,' she said impetuously. 'Flora could come too, and ride. Perhaps your parents. We can, after all, sell the place at any time. Let's enjoy it first.'

'I thought we were going to Sardinia,' he reminded her.

'Ah, that was before I became the lady of the chateau, Vernon. Now I want to come here. Do let's.'

'But of course,' he said. 'Anything the lady of the chateau wants.' He took her into his arms and kissed her. 'You're going to need some living up to, Cristie. I can see that.'

The following morning they again crossed the lawns inside the castle walls for their last ride, for to-morrow morning they would be leaving on the return drive to England. Alastair was saddling the ponies for the two slender, dark-haired boys who were supposed to be helping him but were only succeeding in getting in the way. Firebrand and Countess were all ready to go.

The boys came to be introduced, shaking hands gravely. They were beautiful children with their mother's regular features and dark hair, but their complexions were those of English children, clear and rose-flushed. Angus, the elder, and Neil.

'So you're leaving early to-morrow?' Alastair asked, as he helped Cristina to mount.

'Yes, Vernon says we must be away at the crack of dawn.'

'Then I wonder if you could spare me a few minutes during to-day? For the last few months I had been advising Mrs Marchant about her investments, and there are a few things I should like to explain to you.'

'Certainly, but we have to go down to the notary again this afternoon.'

'Ah, well, I doubt if he'll know enough about the state of the English markets to advise you about investments. What about when you come back? Come and have a drink in the early evening, and I'll have everything ready for you.'

'Early this evening, then.'

Vernon and Cristina left for their ride, cantering comfortably across the plateau; and then Vernon had a fine, exhilarating gallop away from Cristina and back to her, while she sat and waited and admired his horsemanship. The two boys emerged from the stableyard and rode up to Cristina's side, watching Vernon, too.

'He's a super rider,' said Angus.

'Nearly as good as Uncle Alastair,' added the younger one, Neil, for whom obviously nobody could be quite as good as Uncle Alastair.

'Are you going to ride with us?' Cristina asked them.

'No, thank you, we're only allowed to ride on
56

the plateau when we're on our own. Uncle Alastair takes us farther, but your friend is riding his horse —Firebrand.'

' Oh dear, he can't ride because of us.'

' It doesn't matter,' allowed Angus handsomely. ' You're going away to-morrow and then he'll come with us.'

So Vernon and Cristina left them, riding through the crisp cool air of the spring morning. They returned for lunch with Miss Usher and visited the notary later in the afternoon. They had decided to leave Miss Usher in temporary charge of the house, since she seemed to be so capable, and not to tell her of the impending change until their next visit. But when Cristina said to Vernon: ' Well, we'd better go over and see Mr Buchanan about these investments,' he replied quite firmly: ' No, this time, darling, you go by yourself. These are, after all, very private matters.'

' Vernon, I keep telling you. Not private from *you*. I shall only have to come back and tell you what he says.'

' You don't know that. Anyway, you should have the choice, whether you tell me or not. There may come a time, honey, when you'll wish you had kept some things to yourself.'

' I hope not. I want everything to be free and open between us.'

' So do I; but what a girl you are for arguing, Cristie. You aren't frightened of bearding the lion in his den, are you?'

' Good heavens, no! '

' Well, off you go, then.' And Cristina kissed him and left him; to cross the lawn which Alastair Buchanan kept in such good trim, to be admitted by the ever-smiling Marguerite and led to the study where he had first received her. Mrs Buchanan was not in evidence, and Alastair was surprised that Vernon was not, either.

'Mr Walford isn't coming?'

'No. He insisted on my coming alone. He insists that I keep some things private; although of course I shall tell him when I go back.'

'He is indeed a special friend.'

'Yes, indeed.'

'Then he's a lucky man. Now what will you have to drink?'

He poured the drinks, and brought a folder from one of the narrow drawers of an elegant tallboy.

'A word or two of preliminary explanation first,' he said. 'My bona fides, as it were. I suppose I am what one loosely calls a financier. I'm on the board of various companies, a merchant bank and so on; and I manipulate my own assets to increase their value. . . . Now when your grandmother accepted me here as her tenant, she asked me, in her usual brisk and forthright fashion (which I'm sure I don't need to remind you of) what I did for a living. And on hearing what that was, she said that her investments didn't seem to be doing very well, whereupon I offered to vet them for her. And it was immediately apparent to me that there were one or two companies that she should get out of at once; and acting on my advice, she escaped that miserable case of fraud that occupied the press for so long, and also escaped a severe loss.'

He paused to top up their drinks, and went on:

'I won't bore you with a long story, but that raised my status in her eyes and she adopted me as her unofficial adviser in financial affairs. I liked her very much and I believe she liked me—we had some interesting talks. But Miss Usher liked none of it—she wanted your grandmother to herself, she disliked me, and that was why I thought she might have done her best to blacken my household in your eyes. She has tried elsewhere. . . . However, these are the principal things in which I influenced your grandmother.'

He produced various papers which he explained to Cristina until she was completely at sea.

'You'll think I'm dreadfully stupid,' she said at last, 'but really, money matters are an awful mystery to me. Suppose I said that I was perfectly willing to take your advice too? If it was good enough for Gran, I'm sure it's good enough for me . . .'

He smiled then. White teeth in a brown face. Dark eyes under dark hair.

'You see, you should have brought Mr Walford with you. He would have understood.' There was a short pause, before he added: 'But I'm glad you didn't, all the same.'

This surprised her. Surely it was the first personal thing he had said to her, and she realised that she expected only formality from him. He saw her surprise, and added:

'It gives me a better opportunity to get to know you.'

'A very brief acquaintance,' she said, smiling. 'We leave to-morrow.'

'But you will come back?'

'Yes. Yes.'

'Do you know when?'

'Not yet.' She thought he was thinking of his house and what its fate would be. 'Everything at the moment is in the lap of the gods. To sell or not to sell, to keep or not to keep, to sell one house and keep the other . . . To be frank with you, I'd

like to come here for the summer holidays, with
Vernon and friends, of course. In fact, I already
feel, after a few days here, that I could become fond
of the place.'

'That's good,' he said. 'Do you do everything
with Mr Walford?'

'As much as we can,' she admitted candidly.
'We've only known each other about six months
and we both have jobs; but we naturally sort of
gravitate together whenever we're free.'

'You're going to be married? Forgive me, if
that's an impertinent question.'

'I don't really think its impertinent; and we do
expect to get married.'

'Is there a date set?'

'No, we both enjoy the present state of our
affairs. But I *would* think it impertinent if I said
to *you*: Are you going to be married?'

'My answer would be the same as yours. I do
expect to. But the lady in the case simply will not
decide upon a date. May I get you another drink?'

'No, thank you, I must be getting back.' But
she did not move from her comfortable chair.

'So,' he said, looking past her out of the window
at the softly approaching dusk, 'we're both firmly
bound.'

She looked at him quickly, and his dark eyes
came from the window to meet hers. They looked
at each other for long moments, and Cristina was
quite unable to look away. She felt a strong and
certainly to-be-resisted impulse to stretch her hand
out to him. In the silence of the softly-lit room she
felt as if a magnetic attraction was drawing them
slowly together. With an effort, she looked away
and broke the connection forcibly.

'You make it sound as if we're prisoners,' she

said as lightly as she could.

'I think we're probably all prisoners of something or somebody,' he said. 'Prisoners of our families, or of our circumstances. For many people, prisoners of poverty; even prisoners of wealth sometimes.'

'I don't think I'm a prisoner. Once, I admit, I did feel like that; when I lived with my grandmother and wanted to be away. But now I feel free. Before I inherited all this, I mean. I like my job—if I didn't I would change it. I like my affair with Vernon—if I didn't I would put an end to it.'

'Would you?' he asked her. 'Wouldn't loyalty come into it?'

This stopped her. She looked at him and slowly smiled.

'I reserve my answer to that question. I think you're trying to trap me.'

'Not at all. I just wondered how far your freedom really extended.'

'But we're talking about me. What about you? Don't you feel free?'

'Ah,' he said, 'my dear Cristina . . .' and broke off. 'There, I don't even feel free to call you Cristina. May I?'

'Of course. Feel free.'

'Then, Cristina, I have not felt free for a very long time; but I have no intention of embarking on a Buchanan saga so early in our acquaintance.'

'And I really must go,' she said, rising. 'Miss Usher likes an early dinner time.' She smiled at him as they walked towards the door.

She gave him her hand and he took it between both his own, and did not let it go. And Cristina felt that same magnetic force drawing them together. They stood in silence near the door in the softly-lit room, and he said in a low voice:

'If one *were* free to do the things one wants to do . . .'

'What would you do?' she asked softly, and thought, even as she asked it, what a leading question that was.

'I would kiss you,' he said. 'I would wrap my arms about you and kiss you, Cristina. You are so dew-fresh and lovely.'

And she did not move. She did not say: But that's nonsense. With her hand in his, she waited, not even breathless, not even perturbed. And he put his arms around her, so much taller than she was that he almost lifted her off her feet as he kissed her; and Cristina floated away into a world where, for her, the deserts blossomed like the rose and all frustration disappeared. It was peace, sheer peace. And at last he released her and she stood alone, feeling the need of his support; and then, to her own surprise, without knowing what force was so unexpectedly driving her, she said in little more than a whisper:

'As I'm going to-morrow, kiss me goodbye,' and was back in his arms, his lips on hers, her head tilted so far back she thought her neck would break; but bliss all the same, bliss, bliss.

And when he released her this time, he said quietly:

'What price loyalty now, Cristina?'

That awoke her. That brought her back to reality. She stared at him, and shook the dream-like absorption from her eyes and came back to the everyday. What *was* she doing? What had possessed her? She said with sudden forcefulness:

'Oh, it's well to the fore again. Of course, of

course. Goodbye, Mr Buchanan. I must go at once.'

'When you say Alastair,' he said.

'Goodbye, Alastair. And good riddance, Alastair.'

'Never say that,' he protested.

'But I must say it, and must mean it.' She went out of the door.

'Will you come again soon?' he asked of her departing back.

'Who knows? who knows? who knows?' she said as she went along the passage and out of the house; and her voice was light because her heart was light; and her heart was light because Alastair Buchanan had kissed her; and it didn't even seem to be all wrong. It had seemed right, but already she knew it was something that must never be repeated.

Miss Usher and Vernon were in the tower room having their pre-dinner drink when Cristina went in to join them. Vernon glanced at her and then his look intensified and became more watchful.

'Well, how did *you* get on?' he asked.

'Fine, fine,' she replied.

'Sherry for you, Cristina?' asked Miss Usher.

'No, thank you. I had a drink with Mr Buchanan—two, in fact.'

'Perhaps that accounts for a *je-ne-sais-quoi in* your attitude,' said Vernon, still watchfully.

'Could be, Vernon. But it could also be that he's been making lots of money for Grandmother. He's been handling her investments, and it seems with great success. I didn't really understand it all, and as he said, I should have taken you with me. As I tried to do.'

This seemed to reassure Vernon. He relaxed his watchfulness.

'Well, I'm no financial expert,' he admitted.

'You're probably much more knowledgeable than I am, anyway.'

'Well, I should watch him, if I were you,' said Miss Usher, and this was the first word she had allowed herself against him. 'These people who are so clever with money can sometimes overreach themselves. I often wonder why a man whose business is in London buries himself here in this out-of-the-way spot; though of course it could be the irregularity of the relationship in that house that has something to do with it.'

'You mean that he has made a home for his brother's wife and her children?'

'That's one way, and the most charitable, of looking at it. But if you had seen what *I've* seen with my own eyes, you might see it differently. No, there's a lot more going on there than meets the eye.'

'Well, that doesn't concern us,' said Cristina coldly. 'Nor need it concern you in the future either, Miss Usher.' And that promptly reduced Miss Usher to silence, for she had already arranged to stay on here until Cristina's next visit, and hoped to carry on for much longer than that.

Next morning, Cristina was up early, packing. Miss Usher too, had risen early, to give Vernon and Cristina a good breakfast.

'You've made our visit here very comfortable, Miss Usher,' Vernon told her, 'and we've had a wonderful cook.'

'Yes, marvellous meals,' Cristina corroborated. 'I'll let you know when we're coming again, and what eventual plans we have for the house.'

They loaded everything into the car, prepared to leave. As they took the curve of the drive about the round tower, they saw that Alastair Buchanan was walking in the garden. He had a pair of secateurs in his hand and had been, apparently, snipping off dead flowers; but as the car came in sight, he went to the wide gates to open them. In the gateway, Vernon stopped the car.

'Thank you,' he said. 'We're just off.'

'*Bon voyage* to you both, and a quick return. Goodbye, Miss Howard.'

'Goodbye,' she said, wondering at the formal use of her name after last evening. Vernon drove the car through, and Alastair pushed the gates shut after them. Cristina, turning her head, saw that he stood there as long as the car was in sight, watching it until it disappeared. Had he come specially to say goodbye to her? she wondered. Or was it chance that he was in the garden? Was she attaching too much importance to what had happened last night?

They arrived without incident at the Channel port, crossed on a choppy sea and drove straight to Vernon's family to spend the night. They arrived in time for dinner, and at once became absorbed into the wonderfully warm, peaceful, yet lively atmosphere of the Walford house.

'We're all dying to know what you found when you got there,' said Anne. 'Was it, in fact, a chateau?'

'Not what one thinks of automatically as a French chateau,' said Cristina. 'Not all gracious eighteenth century, with turrets and towers.'

'Much older than that,' said Vernon. 'Actually ruined and partially restored.'

'Grim old castle walls, with a lovely round tower and an ancient hall. And inside the walls, two quite livable houses . . .'

'Two houses?' exclaimed Flora.

'Yes, one that Grandmother had; and one is let.'

'And the countryside,' said Vernon, 'is really superb. We had some lovely riding, on borrowed horses.'

'And we already have a plan to have a summer holiday there. Why don't you *all* come?' asked Cristina in an expansive moment.

This caused exclamations and laughter, and the question and answer went on for some time; and with every moment that passed in this familiar and much-loved atmosphere, the spell of that other atmosphere in the old castle walls grew less and less. So that by the time Cristina went to bed that night, she was wondering how she could possibly have behaved as she had. How *he* could have behaved as he had? Was he already feeling as she felt; that it was a moment of unreality, certainly a mistake, and one that he intended not to repeat, as Cristina had already determined?

CHAPTER IV

When Cristina awoke in her own apartment for the
first time since her return from France, she saw the
place in an entirely new perspective. It had always
seemed small to her when she returned to it from
the Walfords' country house, but now, after the
luxury and spaciousness of her grandmother's
French house, and the atmosphere thick about the
castle walls, she saw how mean it really was, how
niggardly the furnishings. True, like most of her
young fellow flat-dwellers, she had tried to brighten
it up with brightly coloured curtains and cushions,
but nothing really disguised the fact that the divan-
by-day was a bed-by-night; that the folding doors
across one end of the room concealed the cupboard-
kitchenette; that the minute bathroom was a
chopped-off piece of the uppermost landing. Yet
in spite of all this, and the worn carpet, and the
cheapness of the furniture, it had often been a
really welcoming small home to her. Nights when
soft flakes of mushy snow fell outside, or fog tried to
creep in by every slightest aperture, it had been
cosy with the gas fire on and the golden-shaded
lamp, and her rented television set to keep her
entertained or informed.

Now, she would gladly hand it over to some
other young adventurer beckoned by the lights of
London. But when she left it, what was she going
to do?

She had arrived at a parting of the ways, and
much depended on Vernon. To marry now? But
he would never live on her money. To marry
later? Which meant finding a new flat. To sell

the chateau, or rent the houses while it appreciated in value? For days on end, these were the questions that filled her mind.

The French lawyers sent her some papers to sign, and she did not quite understand what she would be signing, and took them to Vernon. He discussed them with his father, and neither of them was sufficiently sure about French law to advise her with confidence.

'Go over and see them,' said Vernon. 'They'll explain it to you much better personally. And I daresay Buchanan knows much more about it than we do. He might advise you."

'What? By myself?" exclaimed Cristina.

'Why not? You could go by air and then hire a car. Or better still, drive yourself. You're a good driver.'

'But I haven't got a car,' she protested.

'*Buy* one,' he said, smiling at her look of astonishment as she heard his words.

'Buy one? Just like that? And what do I use for money?'

'Money is the least of your problems, you stupid darling.'

'But I haven't *got* any yet. Not actually money to spend.'

'Your grandmother's solicitors will be very happy to accommodate you, I'm sure. You can go out and buy whatever kind of car you want. Oh, Cristie, I do love you. You're so *un*greedy! Most girls would have started to think of all the things they could buy for themselves.'

'Well, I would like a car of my own,' she said thoughtfully.

'Of course you would. We'll go and buy one for you, darling.'

'Then I could drive myself to the chateau. I *would* like to see it again. I'd like to see if it's as attractive the second time round.'

'Only don't stay away too long, or I shall come and fetch you.'

'Is that a promise? because I'd like you to come again too. But I suppose you have to consider your job.'

'You're darned right I do, if I'm going to support a wife. But I'd sooner lose my job than lose you, Cristie.'

'You don't need to lose either. I won't stay away long.'

They began without delay to look for a car for her; and since their choice was bound by what was in stock and could be had without delay, she found herself the proud possessor of a French car which was comfortable and had a fine turn of speed. And before she had entirely rid herself of the notion that she was living in a fairy tale, she was once more crossing the Channel, calm as a millpond this time, driving the French roads, looking forward to the 'home' village and the castle on top of the cliff.

Some time before she reached it, she was wondering which of the two roads up to the chateau she would take. She regarded the steep and rough shorter way with some apprehension, and had almost decided to go the long way round when her pride came to change her mind, for she thought if Miss Usher could drive that mountainous zig-zagging road, she could too. So she turned her car on to the winding ascent that soon became very steep.

No doubt she would have managed perfectly well, but that on one of the sharpest of the blind corners, she came almost head-on against another car coming down. She jammed on her brakes with such violence that the car skidded on the stones, side-swung towards a low precipice and came to a stop within inches of the edge. Cristina, shaking, made sure she was properly braked and sank back in her seat.

The other car, also braking hard, had landed with its bonnet all but touching the steep cut-away surface of the other side. Alastair Buchanan was out of his car immediately, and walking over to Cristina's side.

'Why Cristina!' His astonishment was obvious. 'What are *you* doing here?'

'Dicing with death, it seems,' she said, her voice still unsteady.

'I'm sorry about that. There's so rarely a car on this road. And this is about the worst stretch, so steep and narrow. But you're all right, I hope?'

'Just,' she said, looking at the narrow margin between herself and danger. 'But scared,' she added candidly. 'Shaking like a leaf.'

'You must let me drive you to the top. You're alone this trip?'

'Unfortunately, yes. Vernon has a job to consider.'

'And how long are you staying?'

'I haven't decided. The lawyers sent me some papers I didn't understand, so rather than discover I had signed away my birthright, so to speak, I thought I should come and see them.'

'If there's anything I can do to help, or explain . . .'

'That's very kind. I would be glad of your help.'

'Well, let me drive you up to the chateau. If you'll move over . . .'

He took a red triangle from the boot of his car,

placed it on the roadway before the bend on which they had almost collided, and returned to take the driving seat of Cristina's car and drive her to the gates of the chateau.

'I'll open the gates for you,' he said, 'and walk back to my car. Welcome home, Cristina.'

'Thank you. It doesn't feel like home.'

'Where is home?' he asked her.

She thought for a moment.

'Nowhere, exactly,' she admitted. 'I have a tiny apartment in London. I suppose Vernon's family house, where I spend most weekends, is more like home to me than anywhere.'

'Ah yes,' he said. 'We mustn't forget Vernon.'

She looked him straight in the eye.

'I don't *want* to forget Vernon, nor have I the slightest intention of forgetting him.'

'Quite right,' he said with a smile. 'And spoken like a queen.'

He opened the car door and went to push open the wide gates. She drove through, but before he closed them again behind her, he went to her window.

'Too late to-day to look at your papers,' he said. 'You must be tired, as well as shaken. I shall be free to-morrow morning.'

'Thank you.'

'And if you want to ride, Countess is at your disposal.'

'Thanks again, but it's really Vernon who's so keen about riding. I don't think I want to go by myself.'

'Well, if you *would* like to ride, I'd be delighted to accompany you. I won't keep you now, Cristina, I'd better go and get my car off the road.'

He closed the gates with himself on the outside,

and Cristina drove to her own front door. That was a loaded conversation, she thought; registering a number of points that had to be made at some time. Alastair had immediately offered to help her with her papers, had offered her Countess to ride, had volunteered to ride with her. All very generous on the part of somebody who was still practically a stranger to her. For her part, she had introduced Vernon whenever possible. Vernon had a job to consider: she had no intention of forgetting Vernon: Vernon was the expert rider: it was Vernon's home which was home to her. She could hardly have made it more explicit that she was utterly committed to Vernon. That should be enough.

Miss Usher had opened the front door and was coming out to meet Cristina. Her smile was friendly.

'Cristina, lovely to see you.' They kissed on both cheeks. 'My word, a new car?'

'Yes, and a French one. Do you like it?'

'It looks splendid, if slightly rakish to my eyes. But did you really need to buy one? Your grandmother's is here.'

'I hadn't really considered that mine. And I had to *get* here. And I could hardly have left you without a car, so far from the village.'

This obviously pleased Miss Usher.

They were taking her bags from the car and carrying them inside.

'It's a wonder the car arrived intact,' Cristina went on. 'Everything was fine until I started up this crazy road; and then I met Mr Buchanan head-on and almost went over the cliff.'

'He does drive like a madman,' said Miss Usher.

'I don't think he was. It was just so very narrow

there.'

'Well, *I* think he drives too fast, and he's very autocratic, as if he expects other people to make way for him. Now, Cristina, I've put you in the same room, and when you've freshened up, there's a drink waiting for you and a *blanquette de veau* for dinner.'

'That sounds super,' said Cristina, wondering why, with such a warm welcome and such splendid attention, she couldn't like Miss Usher more. A nasty little thought would intrude into Cristina's mind: Of course she knows which side her bread is buttered. And she was ashamed of this thought. Perhaps Vernon was right when he said she had a 'down' on poor Miss Usher. Perhaps she, Cristina, had been the jealous one, resenting Miss Usher's influence over her grandmother. She determined she would be nicer to her and less prejudiced, and went downstairs prepared to be both these things.

Drinks in that lovely tower room, sinking into the long, curved, velvet-cushioned couch that fitted against the curved wall. The last of the evening light from outside conflicting with the golden lamps inside. Flowers in beautiful arrangements about the room. Cheese straws melting in the mouth. She raised her glass in silent tribute to all these things and Miss Usher smiled and raised hers, too.

'Your letter said you had to see the lawyers again?' she said.

'Yes. I don't think it's anything important, but I didn't want to sign anything without understanding it perfectly.'

'Very wise, my dear. You should have the best advice.'

'Mr. Buchanan offered to help me.'

'Well, I'm not sure that I would call *his* the best

73

advice.'

'He seems to have done awfully well with Grandmother's investments.'

'Investments are one thing; points of law may be quite another. No, my dear, if I were you, I should rely upon the lawyers.'

'I probably will, but I can hardly refuse Mr Buchanan's help now that it's been offered.'

'Well, as long as you aren't swayed by him.' There was a short pause while Miss Usher gently swirled the liquid round in her glass and made up her mind to speak. 'Cristina,' she said gently, 'I do feel that I should give you a little word of warning.'

'Warning? About what?'

'About the Buchanan family, but especially about Alastair Buchanan. The set-up there is not quite all that it seems.'

'I don't know anything about the set-up there,' said Cristina, and there was a slight edge to her voice, a beginning of coldness in spite of her resolve.

'You know that he is living with his dead brother's wife and children.'

'Yes, I know that; but I don't quite know what you mean by "living with".'

'I mean it in the two most obvious senses. In the sense that they are sharing a house. And that they are living as man and wife.'

'How can you possibly say that, Miss Usher? How can you *know* it?'

'Oh, Cristina, they've been here nearly a year. Do you think I go about with my eyes shut? Or don't hear things the children and Marguerite and the servants say? One would have to be blind *not* to know it. And why do you suppose a man in his position buries himself out here? When he goes to

London on business, he goes alone. They don't go out into any society here, or scarcely any . . .'

'He said that Mrs. Buchanan was very nervous and shy.'

'Of course he would say that.'

'He also said they were going to be married.'

'Well, what's stopping them? *He* may delude the poor creature into thinking he's going to marry her, but just wait until he's interested in somebody else, and see how much truth there is in that.'

'She's so beautiful, she wouldn't have difficulty in finding a husband.'

'She probably *is* in love with him. He's the one who knows he can have her without marriage. Well, I don't want to harp on it. I prefer not to think about them, though it's difficult when they're right on our doorstep. But I thought I should let you know how matters stand.'

'How they seem to *you* to stand, Miss Usher.'

'I've been here longer than you, Cristina. I don't think it will take long for you to see them that way. I just want you to be on your guard. Now let's talk of pleasanter things.'

The pleasanter things centred chiefly round Cristina and Vernon. Miss Usher said:

'I do think he's a most charming young man, Cristina. I'm sure your grandmother—and I myself—would be very happy to see you married to him.'

'Yes, he's absolutely super. And although Grandmother will never see it, you might have the opportunity—not too long delayed—to be very happy, because we've every intention of getting married.'

'Why delay at all, now that you're placed so comfortably?'

75

'Miss Usher, you don't know Vernon. He's modern-minded enough to know that he doesn't have to supply *everything*; but on the other hand, he wouldn't like me to supply everything. So I guess we have to wait until he's in a position to get us a house in England.'

'And that makes me think more highly of him than before. Come, Cristina, let's have dinner.' They put their glasses on the silver tray and made their way to the dining room. 'Yes, he's such a charming young man,' Miss Usher repeated.

So when, next day before lunch, Cristina crossed the lawns towards the Buchanan household, she had all Miss Usher's remarks well docketed in her mind. Miss Usher could be absolutely right, of course. On the evidence presented, it probably seemed to *her* that she was. On the other hand, she could be hopelessly wrong; and Cristina kept an open mind.

Alastair was waiting for her in his study. He was charming but businesslike, devoting himself to her affairs. All was in order, he assured her, except that, on one point, he would have preferred an alteration in the wording to prevent any ambiguity; and if she would allow him, he would accompany her to her lawyers to explain this point. She accepted gratefully. He gave her a drink before she returned to her own house, enquired about Vernon, was correct and quite impersonal. Cristina knew she should be grateful for this, and wondered why it faintly irritated her.

In the afternoon, driving to the lawyer's office, during the interview, driving back, the same charming formality prevailed. As they passed a small restaurant, simple and not too prepossessing, he asked if she had eaten there with Vernon.

'No, Miss Usher provided us with such wonderful meals that it never occurred to us to eat out.'

'But you should eat there. The food is ambrosial, truly out of this world. Why not come there to dinner to-night?'

'I'm sure Miss Usher has already planned something for to-night.'

'To-morrow, then? You can let her know well in advance.'

'But wouldn't Mrs Buchanan object to that?' asked Cristina.

'But she will come too, of course.'

'Then I should love to, thank you.'

'And I will alert Madame Delavent, so that she will give us a meal fit for the gods.'

'I shall look forward to that,' said Cristina.

She did indeed look forward to it, because she found the day strangely long. She missed Vernon, and realised that she wanted him with her. So that as the afternoon drifted past, she really looked forward to the evening.

Dressed in a simple green dress, with a cobwebby shawl over her arm, and the large emerald her grandmother had left her in a ring on her finger, she walked round the tower to the front door where Alastair's car was waiting. Sunset was already streaking the western sky with gold and flame, as he came out through the imposing doorway to greet her.

'All set?' he asked her. 'Then let's go.'

'But where is Mrs Buchanan?' she asked.

'She begs you to excuse her,' Alastair said. 'She has one of her migraine headaches.'

The first doubt assailed Cristina. Had he meant Sylvana Buchanan to come in the first place? Had he even mentioned the small dinner party to her? Or had that been simply the sop to keep Cristina happy?'

'Then I don't think we should go,' she said promptly.

'She's in bed,' said Alastair. 'I should have to eat my dinner alone, so why don't we do as we originally planned?'

'It seems so heartless, when she isn't well,' protested Cristina.

'She assured me that she didn't want to spoil our evening.'

Cristina hesitated, doubtful; but at last said:

'Very well, let's go.'

It fitted in rather too well, however, with Miss Usher's recent warning for Cristina to feel quite happy about it. As they negotiated the tricky downhill road towards the village, she asked:

'Does Mrs Buchanan often have these migraines? I remember she couldn't join us for a drink that first day because of one.'

'I'm afraid she does. She seems to be less settled in health and much more nervy than she used to be.'

'What a pity! She's very beautiful, isn't she?'

'Yes, but with a serious kind of beauty now. When we first knew her—when Angus first brought her to see us—she was absolutely stunning. Smiling and sparkling and gay.'

'Well, losing one's husband and finding oneself alone with three children would be apt to make anyone serious, I suppose,' said Cristina. 'I'm sorry, I didn't mean to be rude or to intrude, because I know she isn't alone now. She has you. But I'm sure you understand what I meant.'

'Quite,' he said drily. 'Marriage to me can hardly be as exciting as marriage to Angus.'

'And I didn't mean that,' said Cristina, distressed. 'You know I didn't.'

They were silent until they reached the small restaurant. It looked very dull from the outside, and Cristina was disappointed to find it almost as dull inside; for the tables and chairs were primitive, the tables covered by simple linen cloths, and the only flowers were wild ones gathered from the hedgerows. But already two tables were occupied and Madame Delavent herself came to welcome Alastair and Cristina.

Cristina soon discovered that the surroundings did not matter. The food was excellent, the wine chosen by Alastair loosened her tongue, and their conversation absorbed her so much that she scarcely even looked around her. Yet afterwards she could not discover anything so absorbing in what was said.

They knew nothing about each other. There was everything to learn. Her grandmother was the link between them. Alastair considered her a remarkable woman, transplanting to France at her age, and taking on the continued restoration of the chateau. 'She was a determined lady,' he said with a smile.

'Yes, I found that out at a very early age, when my indulgent mother went off to the States with her new husband and left me with Grandmother. I suppose I was a fairly determined character, too, so we had rather a rough ride."

'You were a difficult filly to break in,' he suggested. 'Another like Firebrand.'

'Not really, but Grandmother had old-fashioned ideas and strict standards. She had a duty towards me and was determined to do it; and there was nobody to take the pressure off. Just Grandmother and me.'

'Did you never go to see your mother in the

States?'

'Never. It was always going to happen and never did. Travels, pregnancies, children's illnesses—always something to intervene. They didn't really want me, I suppose, or they would have arranged something.'

'Rather unnatural of your mother, surely?'

'I certainly thought so at the time.'

'And there was no Miss Usher then?'

'No, she came along much later. That's another story.'

'Tell me about it.'

So their talk went on: from the advent of Miss Usher to Cristina's descent on London: 'Which made no effect on London, though it did on me. I expect you know a different London. Did you live there until you came to France?'

'I have a house there, yes. I lived and worked there because my real home is far too out of touch with everything.'

'And where is that?' she asked him.

'In Sutherland, far north. The grandest, loneliest countryside, with spectacular cliff scenery and wonderful lakes and rivers for fishing. Bonnie, bonnie Scotland,' he said quietly.

'And you love it there.'

'Yes, I love it there.'

'Why not go *there*, then, if Mrs Buchanan wants to be quiet and remote?'

'Two reasons, Cristina. The first is that my mother still lives in the ancestral home, and she doesn't approve of my marrying Angus's wife. Secondly, Sylvana is Italian and she needs the sun and the warmth, both of which are too transient in Sutherland. Scotland shrivels her up. She isn't made of the stern stuff of Scots.'

They talked of the children too. The little girl Jennifer stayed always close to her mother, but the boys loved Sutherland and liked to go and stay with Alastair's mother. They were beginning to ride well and showed signs of being adventurous. It was obvious to Cristina that he looked forward to training them in all country matters. He would take them fishing on those Scottish lakes, take them tramping the mountains, ride with them, later perhaps teach them to shoot and hunt.

But he did not talk of his brother Angus, and she could not gather how he had felt about him. She wondered briefly if perhaps both brothers had loved the same girl, Sylvana; if Alastair was coming late into his kingdom by marrying her only when her marriage to Angus had produced three children, and when she herself had come to a more serious beauty.

It was late when they rose from the table and went out into the silent sleepy village. Moonlight lay serene over the old stone cottages, blackened the dark shadows of the cliff and highlighted white walls. They walked slowly to the car.

'Would you like to go for a drive, Cristina?'

'I don't think so, thank you. I'd like to go straight back.'

He accepted it without question, and they made the ascent of the steep, winding road.

'But I would like to show you a view which is always beautiful in the moonlight,' he said. 'I usually stop my car on a night such as this, to admire it.'

When they reached the spot, he pulled the car in to the side of the road. 'Not that there'll be anybody else at this time,' he said, and opening his door, stepped out into the cool night and went round to open Cristina's door for her.

It was, as he had said, a calm, beautiful, grey-black-and-silver view which confronted them. The darkness of the bluff descending craggily to the village, dark shapes of woodland set on mist-pearl meadows, the river wide and silver like a satin ribbon thrown down carelessly to loop and wind among them.

'Pure Gothic,' said Alastair. 'All the nineteenth-century engravings one ever knew. But worth stopping for, Cristina?'

'Yes,' she admitted; and shivering a little in the night air, added: 'But rather chilly. I'll get my shawl.'

'Let me get it for you,' he said, and brought it from the car, and placing it round her shoulders, said: 'How can you expect such a fragile spider's web to keep you warm?' and promptly got the gold strap of his wristwatch caught in that spider's web and could not get it free.

'I'm sorry,' he said. 'Hold still a moment, while I disentangle it. I don't want to tear your shawl.'

She waited patiently, but he could not see to get it free.

'Let me,' she said, turning to free herself of the shawl, and turned straight into his arms. It was a very slight collision, that took them both by surprise, but immediately his arms closed round her, and immediately Cristina sank into their warmth and comfort. And it seemed they were straight-away fused together into a close content, a complete satisfaction, and Cristina hoped that he would not move to release her.

She also hoped that he would not kiss her. That would be so definite, so purposeful a thing that it could not be ignored. She would then have to extricate herself, have to put a stop to it. She refused to look at the fact that this embrace was only different in degree. She leaned against him, the pearl and silver of the view forgotten, and loved the strength with which he held her, loved the fact that he was so much taller that she could rest her head so comfortably against his shoulder.

How long they stood together clasped in each other's arms, she did not know. At last he set her free, and only then did they realise that they were still attached to each other because his watch was caught in her shawl.

'Take off your watch, Alastair,' she said, and was grateful to this small *contretemps* for making their descent to earth so natural. 'I'll sort it out.'

They drove to the chateau. At Cristina's own door, she disentangled the watch by the interior light of the car.

'I'm afraid it has torn it,' said Alastair; and both knew they had ignored the shawl in the comfort of being so closely together.

'Never mind, it isn't important,' said Cristina.

'I'll get you another one.'

'No, I'm sure I can fix this one. Good-night, Alastair, it's been a lovely evening.'

'Will you ride with me to-morrow, Cristina?'

'I don't think so. I don't think it would be sensible, do you?'

'Would there be any harm in it, Cristina?'

'There might be,' she said slowly.

'No. I assure you there wouldn't. Cristina, I haven't forgotten anything or anybody. You are committed and so am I. Need that prevent our riding together?'

'Perhaps it should. I don't know. Let me think about it, please.'

'Come to the stables at ten, if you feel like it.'

'And if I'm not there, you will know that dis-
cretion is the better part of valour.'

He took her to the door, and Cristina went
thoughtfully into her own house; but finding Miss
Usher waiting for her, quickly assumed a 'social'
face and a bright smile and said Miss Usher should
not have waited up.

'I'm usually up at this hour, Cristina. Have a
good time?'

'Very. I was a bit surprised to find the place so
homely, but the food was marvellous.'

'Mrs Buchanan didn't go with you, after all?'

'No, she had a migraine and went to bed.'

'Strange! I saw her crossing the garden during
the evening. One doesn't usually recover from a
migraine so quickly.'

'Are you sure?' asked Cristina, surprised.

'Of course I'm sure. I'm hardly likely to mistake
the old cook, or Marguerite, for her. If Alastair
Buchanan told you she was in bed, he told you a lie.'

'I'm sure there's some simple explanation,' said
Cristina, dismissing the matter, but Miss Usher's
sceptical expression did not agree with her.

Nor did Cristina dismiss it as lightly as she had
seemed to before Miss Usher, because she did not
like to think that Alastair had lied; and if he had,
why he had. She did not believe he was the man to
chase a little pleasure on the side, but why else
scheme to take her out without the woman he was
to marry? And if Alastair's behaviour was strange,
what about her own? Was there any difference
between them? She only knew that from the beginning there had been a strong pull between them,
and that now it was heaven to be in his arms. It
was something quite unknown in her brief experi-

ence. It seemed crazy. A small voice in her mind whispered: 'Love at first sight.' She thrust it away and would not listen. She loved Vernon. Vernon had always been special, and she and Vernon were going to marry. No, this strange attraction was but a shooting star, lovely, but gone in an instant.

Next morning she went down to breakfast still undecided whether to ride or not. She was wearing jeans and a sweater—an outfit that would allow her to decide at the last moment. She was glad that Miss Usher was on her way to the village because she did not want to have to talk to her. She wanted to think.

The sum of her thought, as she sat at her solitary breakfast, was that something about this situation was all wrong, and that it must not be allowed to continue. She knew that relationships between men and women never stood still: they were in a state of growing and blossoming, or of decline.

She wondered if she could be making a mountain out of a molehill. What was there, after all, in a casual hug, one kiss lightly given and taken, a handhold in the darkness? Nothing, surely to build a tragic situation upon. And having resolved this, she crossed to the stables at ten o'clock to go riding.

Alastair was saddling Firebrand, but he immediately called to Jean-Pierre, his gardener, stable-boy, handyman, to saddle Countess too. The ponies were brought out too. 'The boys are coming with us,' Alastair told Cristina, and immediately she was filled with reassurance. This seemed to make everything all right, and she enjoyed her morning ride enormously, her mood matching that of the day, which was one of splendid early summer weather, not a cloud in the intense blue of the sky, the sun hot with a southern heat.

Everything seemed even more all right in the afternoon, if by that she meant that there was nothing to worry about. She went to read in the garden outside the castle wall, but after the exertion of the morning ride, fell asleep in the sun. She woke later to the sound of children's voices from the other side of the wall, and closed her book, went through the smaller gateway into the garden between house and stables, and saw that a picnic tea was being arranged upon the grass. Marguerite was being helped by all three children. Angus immediately called to Cristina.

'Are you coming to our picnic?' he asked. 'It's the first one this summer.'

'We're having our tea in the garden,' explained serious, six-year-old Neil.

'*En français, en français,*' cried Marguerite, clapping her hands.

Angus turned to explain to Cristina.

'We always have to speak French when we're with Marguerite. But I don't think it counts when we have visitors. Do you know Marguerite?' he added, with adult politeness.

'Yes, we have met,' Cristina assured him, and smiled at Marguerite, extending her hand to her. '*Comment ça va,* Marguerite?'

There was a lot of chatter, and a lot of arranging and rearranging of the picnic tea. Cristina accepted their invitation to stay, and also accepted orange juice and a sandwich, thinking how little it needed to make children happy. A simple matter of having their food outside instead of indoors, of sitting on the grass and getting it on their patisserie, was enough to delight them. And suddenly Neil cried out:

'Oh, good, here's Mummy! She's coming to our picnic, too.'

Cristina looked up quickly, towards the Buchanan house, and saw that Sylvana and Alastair were coming out together. Alastair had an arm about her, his hand gently resting on her shoulder, and there was something about their attitude—something of understanding and comfort and tenderness —that suddenly pierced Cristina to the heart. It was something that she did not have herself, and she was jealous, unexpectedly and fiercely jealous; and looked away in case it should be visible on her tell-tale face, and then looked back because she could not bear to miss a moment of that picture of them together.

'Why, you have a visitor,' said Alastair, as they came up to the group; and there were greetings, and protests when it seemed that Alastair and Sylvana were going away; until at last they said they would stay.

'But you should offer tea to Miss Howard,' Alastair said. 'Marguerite, will you run to the house and ask Marthe for tea, and Jean-Pierre can bring the garden chairs.'

'No, no,' protested the children. It wasn't a picnic if the garden chairs were brought.

Jennifer shared a rug with her mother, leaning against her, her head against Sylvana's breast, her sticky, cream-smudged fingers on the immaculate ice-blue of the trouser suit, and Sylvana making no objection. Was she always so perfectly turned out? wondered Cristina. Pearls at her ears, rings on her fingers, her hair unruffled. Was her face always so still? Alastair said she now had a serious beauty, where once she had been smiling and sparkling and gay, but did she never now sparkle for him, or smile with any other smile than the grave and tender one she was giving Jennifer now?

The scene was encapsulated for her at that moment: Sylvana smiling down at the contented, nestling Jennifer; Alastair being told what to do by the two lively boys who considered themselves the hosts; Marguerite looking on with her alert and mischievous face ready to break into laughter at any moment. They would be a very happy family, Cristina thought; and wondered, as Miss Usher had the other evening, what was stopping them from becoming one, and also wondered (no doubt instigated by Miss Usher too) if they were in fact already a happy family in everything but name. And the jealousy returned unexpectedly to stab her again.

After the picnic she went for a drive, feeling strangely lonely, once again wishing that Vernon was with her. She returned to have a drink with Miss Usher before dinner, and to watch a television programme after it; but when the telephone bell interrupted it, she went at once to answer. It was Vernon.

'Vernon, how wonderful to hear you! I've been thinking about you.'

'Splendid, I've been thinking about you too, Cristie. How are you getting on?'

'Fine. Everything is settled. The papers were all in order.'

'Good. Are you thinking of coming home?'

Suddenly the thought of going home was vastly attractive.

'Do you want me to?' she asked.

'Do I *want* you to? If you don't come soon, I shall come and fetch you.'

'Of course I'm coming home. There's nothing to stop me. I'll come to-morrow. I miss you,

88

Vernon.'

'Honey! Have you been lonely?'

'Yes.'

'I should have rung you before. I nearly did last night.'

'It was a good thing you didn't. I went out to dinner.'

'Who with?'

'Alastair Buchanan.'

'Just the two of you? Not Mrs Buchanan?'

'No, she had a migraine.'

'Again?'

'Again.'

'So you haven't been lonely, Cristie?'

'In one way, no, because I went riding this morning, too . . .'

'With Buchanan, of course.'

'*And* the boys—a very family affair. And they had a picnic this afternoon and invited me—another very family affair. But that didn't stop me being lonely for *you*.'

'Oh, come home, Cristie, come home.' And there was an urgency in his voice that awoke a response in her.

'All right, darling, I'll start to-morrow, and drive straight to your family's house, if they'll put up with me. And you come down on Friday evening. That's only three days away.'

'Of course the family will put up with you. Especially Flora. You've practically committed yourself now, Cristie. She quite thinks she's going to your chateau for the holidays, riding, and boating on the river and having a wonderful time.'

'Well, I meant it. We'll all do it, Vernon.'

They talked until Cristina said the telephone bill would ruin him, and when she went back to the salon, her heart was lighter, and her mind made up; and she said sunnily to Miss Usher: 'That was Vernon. I think I'll go home to-morrow, Miss Usher.'

She had an idea that Miss Usher was definitely pleased by this piece of news. Perhaps she liked having the comfortable house within the castle walls to herself. Perhaps it was because she seemed to approve of Vernon so much while disapproving equally of Alastair Buchanan. Or it could be that she was glad and relieved still to be in her post. But Cristina had no time for Miss Usher at the moment. She went upstairs to pack, determining on an early start next morning.

Miss Usher was up, resolved that Cristina should start her long drive with a good, sustaining breakfast.

'I shan't need lunch after all this,' declared Cristina.

'I daresay you will, by early afternoon. When do you think of coming again?'

'I don't know. The one definite thing is that some of Vernon's family are coming here with me for summer holidays. I don't know if I need to come before then.'

'Just let me know and I can have everything ready for you. And your friends.'

There was a short silence. Miss Usher wondered if she had taken too much for granted. Cristina knew that she did not really want Miss Usher to be housekeeping for them all then. But now, when she was anxious to be away, was not the moment to go into all that. She said:

'Well, I'm off now. Don't bother to come out, Miss Usher.'

Miss Usher came out, however, saying she would

open and close the gates, and stood waving to the departing car before she walked back by the round tower to the house; and was glad of the solitude, and cleared away the breakfast dishes and lovingly polished the dining table, and put Cristina's bedroom to rights, until the house was once more as she loved it, as she and Mrs Marchant had shared it.

So once more Cristina drove along a route which, although not yet familiar to her, already had distinguishing landmarks; once more crossed on the car ferry, on to familiar roads that led her to Vernon's home. And there was Vernon to greet her.

'But you shouldn't be here until to-morrow,' she protested.

'I had a day off, by cramming two visits in yesterday instead of one, and working an eighteen-hour day. There's devotion for you!'

'Well, *I* drove all day. Not eighteen hours, I couldn't do that; but a long, long time, to get back to you.'

'That's more devotion than I deserve.' They were walking into the house, an arm about each other, their spare arms carrying the bags; and the moment they were inside the hall, deserted at that moment, they dropped the bags and were in each other's arms, kissing with a passion and intensity that were increased by the short separation: increased too, perhaps, by a faint feeling of guilt in Cristina and a stirring jealousy in Vernon. They clung together and wordlessly renewed their vows to each other, their passionate kisses re-dedicating themselves to each other.

CHAPTER V

During the next few happy weeks Vernon and
Cristina made plans, altered them, made new ones,
and endlessly discussed their future. At weekends
they drove down together to Vernon's home; during
the week there were parties and meetings with
friends, films, and suppers in moderately comfortable but inexpensive restaurants. There was little
to indicate that Cristina had newly inherited a
small fortune.

The inheritance became apparent when Cristina
talked of changing her flat.

' I don't want to stay cooped up here much longer,'
she said, ' but is it worth changing, if we're going
to look for a house in the near future?'

' If you got a bigger flat, we could always keep
it going until we found a house,' Vernon replied.

' And there's another thing. How much time
would I spend in France? and if it's only a short
time each year, is it worth keeping *that* on? It
isn't, really. And if it were sold, we could have a
super house over here.'

' But not bought with your money, Cristie.'

' Vernon, that's so old-fashioned, darling. What
does it matter *whose* the money is? What's mine
is yours.'

' Cristie, you're sweet, but I can't get married
owing everything to you.'

And so their arguments proceeded, and usually
ended with their arms around each other, with
passionate kisses, with a putting-off of any decision
until some other time.

One plan that was adhered to was the one for a

family holiday at the chateau. At first, only Flora and her parents intended to accompany Vernon and Cristina, but later Anne and Ralph each decided to fly over for a visit, curious about the chateau and longing to see it. Cristina resolved to write to Miss Usher to explain that her services were no longer needed, and to thank her for the years she had spent with Mrs Marchant.

It was an extremely difficult letter to write. She spent a long time over it, making it as tactful as she could, but she knew that, however it was couched, it would still be unwelcome to Miss Usher. But Cristina had already discovered that Miss Usher still owned her pretty cottage in Grandmother's village, and that it was let to an American family on a six-month basis. So she was far from being homeless; and added to her own means was the amount of five thousand pounds which Grandmother had left to her, besides the 'gifts' of jewellery which had considerable value.

'I don't know why you should feel guilty,' Vernon said. 'If you don't like her, don't keep her. It was your grandmother who employed her. And Miss Usher had no compunction about driving *you* out when it suited her. And remember, Cristie, she had rent for her furnished cottage for six years while she was living in great comfort with your grandmother. It seems to me she's come out of it very well.' All the same, Cristie was glad when the letter was posted, although she half expected a long letter of protest in reply. When one did not arrive, she did not know whether it made her anxious or relieved.

One midweek evening when Vernon was out of town on business, Cristina began to tidy the crammed drawers of her desk. She had hardly

93

started on the work, a radio programme making a gentle hum to keep her company, when the bell of her flat rang, and she opened the door to discover Alastair Buchanan on the half-dark of the landing.

'Good evening,' he said seriously, watching her reaction.

'Good heavens!' she replied. 'Well, this is unexpected.'

'Unexpected, but not unwelcome, I hope?'

'Of course not. Come in, to my palatial home.'

He came in, seeming to dwarf the low-pitched room with his height. He looked so handsome and elegant that Cristina was glad that everything in this mini-apartment was clean and tidy: it certainly had little else to recommend it. The divan cover was straight and its many cushions plumped up. Fresh flowers were on the coffee table and the peculiar piece of furniture that served as a sideboard. The doors covering the cupboard kitchen were closed. It was as spruce as it could ever be.

'Do sit down,' Cristina said. 'I suppose business brought you over?'

'Yes, I've been busy all day. I wouldn't have come unannounced, but I couldn't find you in the book.'

'No, you wouldn't. I share a telephone and it's not in my name.'

'I wondered if there was a remote possibility that you would have a free evening, and that I might persuade you to have dinner with me. Also, I came to bring you this.' And 'this' was a flat parcel, gift-wrapped. Cristina took it from him and asked if she might open it at once, and found inside a shawl even more cobwebby than the one he had torn on his wristwatch, made by hand with infinitely fine wool, probably by remote Shetland

Islanders, in a complicated lacy pattern. 'The sort they always tell you can be drawn through a wedding ring,' said Cristina, admiring it at arm's length. 'It's beautiful, but it really wasn't necessary to replace the other. I managed to mend it.'

'I'm afraid it's more ornamental than useful, but I did promise to replace the other. I'm not going to be so rash, however, as to help you with this one.'

For a moment they both remembered the circumstance of the other shawl being torn, and both preferred to forget it. Cristina said:

'May I offer you a drink? My stock is rather limited, I'm afraid. I keep forgetting I could be more lavish, and go on in the old style.'

'And how long will you do that, I wonder.'

'Ah, if one but knew the answer to that! Vernon and I are for ever discussing the future. But of course I won't stay here. This was all I could afford on my magnificent salary. Well, what will you have?'

They had a drink together and Cristina confessed that that evening was a free one.

'Vernon is out of town on business.'

'Would he mind if I took you out to dinner?'

Cristina thought that he would mind, but she said:

'I'm still a free agent. I would be pleased to come to dinner. Should I change?'

'No. We won't go anywhere where dress is so important.'

They went to dinner in a small and crowded restaurant where the food was excellent and the bill was staggering; and their conversation was fairly superficial and ordinary since it seemed little could be said without being heard by people at neighbouring tables. But when they emerged into the night air and Alastair hailed a taxi to take her home, he invited himself for a good-night drink in her apartment. The golden lights made it a more acceptable place than in daylight. Cristina brought two brandy glasses and the bottle, and Alastair poured it out. 'I don't run to a decanter,' she apologised.

'I shall buy you one,' he said, 'for being so neighbourly as to enliven what could have been a dull evening.'

He was seated on the divan, leaning against the piled cushions. Cristina sat in the small armchair by the coffee table, leaning back and sipping her brandy.

'We were all so disappointed,' Alastair said, 'when we discovered you had gone away from the chateau. We had had such a good day the day before, with the riding and the picnic. It was a very sudden departure, wasn't it?'

'Yes. Vernon telephoned me that evening; and he was missing me and I was missing him. So!'

'Then we obviously couldn't compete. The boys wanted you to ride again, and Jennifer picked you a posy of wild flowers. That was how we found out you had gone. She went with Angus to give you her bouquet. It was very brave of them, because they're in awe of Miss Usher.'

'I can't imagine *her* being fond of children. Actually, I've written to her, telling her not to stay on at the chateau. She's a wonderful housekeeper, but I never liked her personally.'

'The chateau could well be a pleasanter place for her going. How is she placed?'

'Very well. I don't worry on that score. I'm sorry the children were disappointed, but I shall be coming in late June and perhaps they will ride with us then. Vernon and in fact all his family are quite mad about horses.'

'The boys will look forward to that.'

'You aren't going away yourself?'

'Apparently not. I've suggested a number of places to Sylvana, but she prefers to stay where she is. I, of course, will go to Scotland, for the glorious twelfth, whether she comes or not.'

'You're a hunting, shooting and fishing man?'

'Yes. It's part of my upbringing and my heritage. You don't think I'm a rustic, bucolic oaf because of that?'

Cristina laughed outright.

'That description hardly fits you,' she said. 'But why, Alastair, is Sylvana so retiring? It can't all be losing your brother Angus, surely? People do recover from such blows.'

'I wish I knew the answer to that, Cristina. She grows more retiring, instead of less so. I could never get her to fix a date for our marriage, but now it seems she doesn't even want to talk about it. But when I ask her if she has changed her mind, if she wants her freedom in a house that I would provide for her, why, then she gets almost panic-stricken, and throws herself into my arms and begs me not to leave her. It's obvious that the thought of being on her own again simply terrifies her; yet she won't set a date for the wedding. If I didn't know my brother Angus so well, I should imagine there was something about marriage itself that held terrors for her; but Angus was gentle and loving, a much kinder and more considerate person than I am. They considered the arrival of each of their children a great blessing. They loved them all, and each other. . . . I can only think there's something about me which she can't reconcile herself to, though God knows what it is!'

'That's not a very happy position to be in, Alastair.'

'Indeed not. I had no intention of staying in France so long. We went to indulge a whim of Sylvana's, because she was anxious to get away from London. And now she won't come back to England.'

'Perhaps you're indulging her too much.'

'She's so changed. If you could have seen her when Angus first brought her to us, up in Sutherland. She was a radiant creature. We all loved her. She chattered and sang, she sparkled. And when she was quiet, she seemed to give off a glow. That girl can't have disappeared for ever. Something or somebody must be able to bring her back.'

Cristina was silent. Perhaps that girl had disappeared for ever, she thought, all her love and sparkle gone with her young husband, Angus, into the grave. And Alastair, who had just said 'we all loved her' could be setting himself a hopeless task, crying for the moon, in trying to bring her back.

Alastair said:

'But why burden you with my troubles? It's unpardonable. Perhaps by the time you come in June, we shall present you with a *fait accompli*.'

'With a ready-made family.' Cristina smiled. 'I know you're fond of your brother's children.'

'Especially of the boys. Jennifer is a mummy's baby and I think always will be. They're quite inseparable.'

'Well, tell the boys I expect some expert tuition in riding when next I come to France.'

'Yes. And now I must leave you, Cristina. Thank you for your pleasant company.' They went together to the door. 'Good-night.'

Cristina opened the door for him. 'Tonight,' he said, 'common sense prevails. There's no moonlight tonight.'

They shook hands.

'I told myself there was no harm in it,' Cristina said. 'I told myself it was lovely and fleeting, like a shooting star.'

'That almost sounds like an invitation, Cristina; but I think there *was* harm in it. There was the harm that it might happen again and then again . . .'

'It might happen now,' she said, and wondered at herself for saying it.

'You might think then that it was all I came for.'

'And what did you come for, Alastair?'

'To bring you the shawl. No, damn it, I came to see you, to hear your voice, to watch the changing expressions of your face. Perhaps to confirm that I didn't dream you. The shawl was my excuse.'

'It sounds as if it was a shooting star for you, too.'

He shook his head.

'Moonshine, Cristina. Moonshine. But one should keep out of the moonlight, it misrepresents everything. Goodnight.' And with no more farewell than that, he went down the steep, narrow flight of stairs, and left her bereft at the top. Bereft and disappointed, feeling empty and cheated. She turned slowly back into the room, knowing that she had longed to feel his arms about her, wondering, in the intensity of her disappointment, why he had come at all if he had decided they must remain at arm's length. To hear her voice, he had said, to watch the changing expressions of her face. Well, if that was enough for him, it was not enough for her.

Then she realised what she was thinking, and with a feeling of revulsion, she sank down on the divan with her face in her hands, repenting, repenting. It would have been better if he had not come at all. She must take herself in hand. She must somehow exorcise this magnetism that he had for her, though how it could be done she had no idea. She knew that her future, her golden future, lay with Vernon. There was really no sense delaying their marriage, waiting until he could afford to get them a home. She must make him see it her way, that everything they possessed they possessed in common. They must get married soon.

The immediacy of the problem, however, soon lessened, and had vanished by the time she saw Vernon again. She was back to normal, greeting him with her usual delight, falling rapturously into his arms. When he suggested going out to dinner, she said everything was ready for a delicious meal in the apartment. She had time to cook properly now that she had left her job, and a casserole of lamb cutlets, among other good things, was waiting for them. They would have a drink first.

They were ensconced comfortably on the divan with their drinks in hand, Cristina leaning back against the heaped-up cushions, with her legs tucked up under her, when the apartment bell rang. They glanced at each other in surprise.

'Expecting anybody?' asked Vernon, and Cristina shook her head, wondering with a sudden leap of her pulses if it might be Alastair Buchanan again.

Vernon went to open the door and Miss Usher was there on the landing.

'Miss Usher! Hallo, what a surprise. Cristina, here's Miss Usher. Do come in, please.'

Miss Usher came in, glancing about her and obviously very surprised to see the place Cristina was living in. Cristina unfolded herself from her comfortable position and stood up. Her pulse was still beating rapidly, but now for a different reason. She wondered if Miss Usher had come to make trouble.

It did not seem so. Miss Usher's smile was friendly.

'We didn't know you were in England, Miss Usher. Do sit down. You're in time to join us for a drink. I'm afraid I haven't got Pernod, but will you have a glass of sherry?'

'Thank you.' Miss Usher seated herself in the small armchair, and waited for the sherry which Vernon brought her. She noticed that he was at home here, that he assumed the duties of host. She thought they behaved like a married couple.

Vernon and Cristina were both wondering why Miss Usher was here, but Cristina would not ask. She was waiting for Miss Usher to make the first move, and it seemed the politenesses and pointless talk would never end; but at last Miss Usher said:

'I was surprised to get your letter, Cristina; and I must say, very disappointed.'

She paused, waiting, and at last Cristina replied:

'Yes, well, I'm sorry. But Vernon and I have decided on certain plans now.'

'You're going to sell the chateau?'

'Very probably . . .'

'I do hope, Cristina, that you have not found me wanting in any respect? I've done my best to keep everything in the pink of condition, just the way dear Mrs Marchant would have approved of.'

'I know. Everything always looks beautiful. I have no complaints on that score. You've been a wonderful housekeeper and a wonderful cook.'

'I was considerably more than housekeeper and cook to your grandmother,' Miss Usher said with a touch of stiffness. 'I was her companion, and I like to think, her friend.'

'Of course, Miss Usher; but that was my grandmother. Things have changed now.'

'Alas, alas. They were such happy days.' Miss Usher looked sadly into her glass of sherry for a few seconds before looking at Cristina again. The charm came back to replace that momentary sadness, but Cristina did not trust that assumed charm. 'But I think you told me, Cristina, that you were having a summer holiday at the chateau with Mr Walford's family. Is that still true?'

Cristina had to admit that it was.

'Then surely you'll need a housekeeper for that period? I would be happy to take all the catering and work off your shoulders, and leave you free to enjoy your holiday.'

'That's very kind of you, Miss Usher, but my plans are made now. I think we'd better leave it, as I wrote to you, that you will leave the chateau at the end of the month.'

Miss Usher looked appealingly at Vernon.

'Can't you persuade her, Mr Walford, to change her mind? To give me a little longer in the house I love so much, the house that is really my own creation? I could save her a great deal of work when you are all there on holiday—and you know yourself what my cooking is like.'

Vernon glanced towards Cristina. This seemed to him a perfectly reasonable request.

'What do you think, Cristie?' he asked her. 'That does seem rather a good idea.'

Cristina saw that Miss Usher immediately looked

hopeful, but she shook her head.

'No. I've decided now. I don't need a permanent housekeeper there.'

'If you're thinking of the expense, Cristina, I do realise that your grandmother paid me a generous salary, and I would willingly stay on for a little less.'

'I'm sorry, Miss Usher. I'm sorry.' Cristina found this interview embarrassing. 'I just don't need a housekeeper.'

'And that's final?'

'Quite final, I'm afraid.'

There was a long silence. Miss Usher put her sherry glass down on the coffee table and gathered up her gloves and bag.

'You won't change your mind, Cristina?'

Cristina shook her head.

'I realise you love the place, Miss Usher, but my grandmother is dead now, and there's no longer a job for you; and you've had a great deal of pleasure and satisfaction from it.'

Miss Usher looked at Cristina and realised that her decision really was final. Between them lay the memory of those former years when Miss Usher had planned and schemed to oust Cristina. Miss Usher said bitterly:

'I put all my efforts into that place. The pleasure and the satisfaction were your grandmother's. It was *my* ideas, *my* energy, *my* plans, that turned it into the place it is today. I did it for your grandmother: not for you to enter into.'

'*I* can't change the course of events, Miss Usher. And you do have your own charming cottage to go to.'

'And you can't be rid of me quickly enough!' Suddenly, Miss Usher threw her friendliness and tact overboard. 'After all that I did there! After the years I spent with your grandmother!'

As if in reply to Miss Usher's bitterness, Cristina abandoned her own efforts at tact.

'Well, you had those years, Miss Usher, in beautiful surroundings, provided for and secure. Look around you at my beautiful surroundings. I've been living in this shabby doll's house and providing for myself. I don't think you've got anything to grumble about.'

'I daresay you had other compensations.' Miss Usher's voice was more than bitter now. It was vindictive. 'You call it a doll's house, but even a doll's house is endurable when it's shared with a lover!'

Cristina's eyes opened wide in surprise at this sudden attack.

'Oh, don't be stupid,' she said at last.

'Really, you must think people are blind,' went on Miss Usher. 'Do you think I don't recognise what's under my eyes? You make a perfect picture of young love, don't you? It's perfectly obvious to me that you're living here together. Just as it's obvious why you want me out of the way at the chateau. So that you can carry on there as you do here, without the awkwardness of people there to witness it. Do you think I believe that his family is having a holiday there? Not a bit of it. If I'm out of the way, you can do just as you like.'

'Miss Usher,' said Vernon calmly, placating her, 'I am *not* living here with Cristina. It wouldn't be very comfortable anyway with one narrow divan between the two of us. I simply came here after a hard day's work to have dinner in the apartment— something that thousands of young people must be doing at this very moment all over London. You may not approve, but customs have changed since your young days.'

'Ha!' she countered, and it was almost a snort. 'You think that *that*'s going to convince me. You don't remember that I saw you both coming out of Cristina's bedroom together on the very first morning at the chateau? And you don't need to tell me again that customs have changed, that bedrooms are no longer sacred. *I* know what's going on. Well, all I can say is that you're going to the right place. You'll be a perfect match for the Buchanans. Like to like. The two of them living as man and wife, and nothing to stop them getting married. And you two! Just imagine the adventures: you'll be changing partners before you know where you are. Well, you all deserve each other. I shall be well out of it!'

Cristina crossed to the door and opened it.

'I'm glad you've come round to that way of thinking,' she said icily. 'You'll be well out of it. There's nothing to detain you right now. I should get out of this polluted atmosphere as soon as you can.' Miss Usher rose to her feet. 'And perhaps the pollution will go with you,' added Cristina blandly.

Miss Usher crossed to the door.

'I shall be out of the chateau at the end of the month. Don't worry about that! I don't think I could bear to be *in* it with you two. I loved that place. Every piece of furniture I've lovingly polished and cared for. Every copper pan in the kitchen I've cleaned until it shone. Perhaps it's a good thing I won't be able to see the pigsty you'll make of it.' She paused again at the threshold. 'By rights, it should have been mine,' she said bitterly. 'Your grandmother said so over and over again, but she never got round to changing her will. You don't deserve it and you don't deserve to be happy there. I hope you won't be.' And with that parting thrust she went across the landing and down the stairs, leaving Cristina at the open door and Vernon just behind her.

Slowly, Cristina closed the door. Slowly turned to face Vernon.

'Well, there's your poor, lonely lady for you,' she said.

She sounded dejected. She did not like scenes. Vernon closed his arms around her, caressing her, rubbing his cheek gently across her hair.

'You were right about her, Cristie. She managed to behave well as long as it was in her own interest to do so. But now she's gone. Don't worry about her. We *will* be happy at the chateau, darling, I promise you.'

Cristina clung to him, turning her face up to kiss him and being passionately kissed in return. Then, arms still entwined about each other, they walked across the room to the small dining table.

'Let's have this casserole that smells so good,' said Vernon, and they released each other, kissed lightly and gently on the lips, and turned their attention to getting dinner.

'Usher sounds as vindictive about the Buchanans as she was about us,' Vernon commented, as they ate.

'Probably with as little truth,' said Cristina.

'Probably,' agreed Vernon.

'They seem an attractive family,' said Cristina, 'and it will be nice for all of us to have them as neighbours when we go there. We can ask them to visit us. Oh, it will be much friendlier without Usher there.'

'Did she really think your grandmother would leave the house to her?'

'Wishful thinking. I certainly can't see Grandmother doing it. I don't think Miss Usher has much respect for the truth. I don't believe Grandmother gave her the jewellery, but there's nothing I can do about it. I'm glad she's gone. Let's forget her.' This they proceeded to do, and the atmosphere, rather than being polluted as Miss Usher's remarks had suggested, seemed more clear and free now that they were rid of her.

Then the day arrived when Cristina prepared to drive through France to the chateau once more. She had given up her mini-apartment and removed her few personal possessions to Vernon's family home in the country, where the attics already accommodated several generations' throwouts. She felt strangely footloose and fancy free, her only home now her grandmother's French chateau, until Vernon could afford and find a house.

Cristina wanted to go first to have everything in readiness for the Walfords; but when, after an uneventful journey, she reached the house, she was dismayed to find that it did indeed need somebody's loving care. However well Miss Usher had left it, it had accrued a layer of dust since then, and all the beds needed making up after Cristina had aired the sheets. She found that she did not know how to work the boiler and there was no hot water. There was plenty of food in the deep freeze but no everyday provisions such as bread and milk. She would have to find out where the shops were. She was more than grateful to know of the existence of the Buchanans within the castle walls; and decided to go and ask Alastair's advice without delay, about starting the boiler.

She crossed the lawns on the inside of the walls, and Marguerite saw her from the house and came to a side door to greet her, exclaiming with delight, pleased to see Mademoiselle Howard back again.

Yes, Monsieur was here, Marguerite would inform him at once. Cristina waited, and found that at the sound of his step her pulses started that racing that seemed inevitable. She was never sure how he would greet her, but he proved to be, on this occasion, so stiff and formal that she found herself apologising for her intrusion before she explained her errand.

'It's the work of a moment to get the boiler going,' he said. 'I'll come across and show you.' They began to walk to Cristina's house as she asked him how she could find out if there was anybody in the village who would come to work in the house for the next few weeks. 'Vernon's family will be coming in relays, the first three of them quite soon, and I really could do with some help.'

'I shouldn't think that would be too difficult. There's no work for women in the village except housework or helping their husbands in the fields. I'll ask Marthe, who knows everybody, and who will know who is reliable.'

'Thank you very much.'

The boiler was set going without any difficulty and Alastair asked in what other way he could help her. His formality, which was new and strange to her, put her off. She felt slightly embarrassed, even awkward, as if she were intruding into this handsome, elegant man's privacy.

'Only a little advice about the shops,' she said. 'Where one buys everything.'

'I'm sure that Marthe will advise you much

better about all that than I can,' he said. 'I will send her over to see you. I'm sure she will be most helpful.'

And he was gone, without any of the friendliness she had encountered before, without any enquiry about herself, without saying he was pleased that she was back. As she watched him walk to his own house across the lawn, a tall, dark man, well-dressed without sacrificing comfort, a man with superlative ease of manner, she could only think that he had decided that their previous encounters had been unwise, and was putting a stop to any possibility of a repetition. His matter-of-fact coldness had hurt her. She would have preferred it if he had come out into the open, saying: 'We have to be sensible, Cristina, because we are both committed, and it would be better if we both forgot about shooting stars and moonshine.'

Marthe came to see her and offered to go to the village with her next morning and introduce her to the shopkeepers. She also thought her cousin, a woman of forty-five with a growing family, the eldest of whom would be able to look after the younger ones, would welcome the opportunity of earning extra money. 'She's a good cook and a good housekeeper,' said Marthe, 'but she will want to go home every night.'

So, in fact, everything was arranged. Louise would arrive every morning in time to prepare breakfast (probably travelling with the *croissants*) and would be taken home each evening after preparing dinner, by Cristina or a deputy.

'When *I* was young,' Marthe said, as they drove back towards the chateau, 'I would have had to *walk* up this hill every morning, and back every night. They didn't pick you up in motor cars in those days. And she's asking quite enough for her wages, too.' But Cristina was happy to leave the dusting and polishing to Louise, and the making of the beds and the debates with the butcher. The three days in which she waited for the arrival of the Walford parents and Flora seemed to stretch out interminably. There was only one sign from the other house, and that came, not from Alastair, but from the children; since Jennifer wanted to bring her a bunch of flowers and the two boys accompanied her. They came in eagerly, chattering excitedly, and she gave them milk and biscuits, glad to see them; but before long Marguerite arrived to take them away, scolding them for staying too long. In vain did Cristina protest that she liked them to come; in vain did she wait for a sign from Alastair. She did not even see him working in the garden. He seemed to be avoiding her, and it worried her. She felt strangely desolate, realising that she had been looking forward to friendship with the Buchanan family at the chateau.

So that when the Walfords arrived, putting an end to her loneliness, she welcomed them with great delight. It was gratifying to see their reaction to the outside of the chateau, exciting to show them everything, to explain all that had been done, to show them the round tower room and know that they appreciated its age and beauty.

Suddenly the house came to life. Even when she had been here with Vernon it had not come to life, because there had been something repressive about Miss Usher, something that suggested she was watching every beloved piece of well-polished furniture, waiting to remove the slightest finger-mark, apprehensive about the slightest scratch. The Walfords, accustomed to beautiful but comfortable houses, were immediately at home in this one, and Cristina's loneliness vanished, her serenity returned. Mr Walford, unfolding his long length from the deep velvet chairs and sofa, Mrs Walford showing a surprising facility in French as she discussed menus with Louise, even Flora, all impatience to go over to the Buchanans' stables, filled her with the contentment of having familiar things around her. To Flora, she said:

'They're not *my* stables, Flora. At least, I suppose I own them, but they are let to the Buchanans. And the horses belong to the Buchanans. I can't really go without an invitation.'

'Can't you just ring them up and ask if I can go over and *see* the horses? They wouldn't mind that, would they?'

Cristina was strangely reluctant to ask anything of the now-distant Alastair, but promised to ring him up next morning, and at breakfast next day was promptly reminded of her promise by Flora.

It was Alastair himself who answered the telephone and listened to Cristina's slightly embarrassed request.

'But of course,' he said immediately. 'Let her come whenever she wishes.'

'You don't know Flora,' Cristina told him. 'She would be living there if I told her that.'

'Is she a good rider?'

'Oh, she's a natural. She'd rather be in a saddle than anywhere.'

'In that case, perhaps she would like to ride. She's welcome to Countess.'

'That's *very* kind of you, though I expect she'd adore to ride Firebrand. But for this morning, we'll content ourselves with just looking. Thank you very much.'

'You're welcome, Cristina,' he said pleasantly. Pleasantly, but without warmth, she thought, as she rang off. Pleasantly, but distantly. Unaccountably, unreasonably, she felt rejected.

After breakfast, all four of them walked across the wide lawns to the stables, Mr Walford also interested to see the horses, and his wife more interested in the layout of Cristina's property. Jean-Pierre was saddling the ponies. Apparently the boys were going to ride.

'Oh, aren't they darlings!' exclaimed Flora, immediately patting and stroking, at home in what seemed to be her natural element. She went on to Countess and then to Firebrand, talking to him, laughing at his snorting, not in the least surprised when he ceased his fidgeting and recognised her as a friend.

Angus and Neil arrived, dressed for riding, never allowed on a pony without the hard black velvet cap. And hard on their heels came Alastair. There were introductions all round, conversation broke out spontaneously, without any awkwardness, any embarrassment, Alastair a perfect host, the Walfords perfect guests. And before they separated, Alastair had asked them all to have a drink with him that evening and the Walfords had accepted with pleasure.

So, thought Cristina, the formality is only for me, not for anybody else. He is probably delighted to have congenial company, thankful for the opportunity to entertain his compatriots. It is only for me, this aloofness, this stand-offish attitude. He has thought better of that quicksilver, magnetic relationship. He has re-committed himself to Sylvana. But it was a pity, she thought, that it seemed to mean the end of a friendship, too.

The evening meeting confirmed what she thought. He was charming. The Walfords were obviously delighted with him. Sylvana was there, shy, very quiet, but more natural than Cristina had yet seen her. Still impeccably dressed, always with jewels at her ears and on her fingers, looking to Alastair for support from time to time, and still leaving all the entertainment to him. And he was equal to it. The only fault that Cristina could find was that he was stiff and formal to her, spontaneous to all the others. He might have been meeting *her* for the first time. Everything that had gone before had been completely wiped away; and perhaps she should have been glad of that fact, but it left her feeling the poorer, feeling deprived.

CHAPTER VI

Because of Alastair's extreme formality, at least as far as she was concerned, Cristina was all the happier to welcome Vernon, when he arrived three days later. Certainly he had no cause to complain, since she flew into his arms in the comfortable hallway, holding herself closely to him, kissing him ardently and then saying: ' Oh, darling, it's lovely to see you! ' They went into the tower room with their arms about each other, and Cristina's face was radiant. It needed but one glance from the others to see that Cristina's spirits, which had seemed a little low for a day or two, had completely recovered.

It was true that she had felt despondent and rejected by Alastair's coolness towards her, and true that she found compensation for it in Vernon's love for her. Alastair had so obviously chosen the way he must follow, and she must do the same. She must forget that strange, and yet still haunting, interlude.

She and Vernon did everything together. They rode together, having been invited by Alastair to make use of Countess and Firebrand. They went by car down to the village on shopping expeditions, and sometimes farther afield to explore. With the other Walfords they rowed on the river, and swam occasionally in the cold river water. Cristina sat on the bank while Vernon and his father fished, and the whole family went on sightseeing expeditions, complete with lavish picnics.

For the three Buchanan children, Cristina's house was a magnet. So little happened to vary the pattern of their days that they were very excited by the arrival of guests in the other house, and constantly came to visit on one excuse or another. Marguerite was continually coming to take them back, although Cristina and the Walfords protested that the children were welcome. Vernon took the boys on the river, and the family took them, with a picnic, to visit some famous caves. When Alastair and Sylvana came to have an evening drink, Alastair apologised for the fact that they were such a nuisance.

'Of course they're not a nuisance,' Cristina protested. 'They're charming boys, we all love them.' And for a moment there was a smile round Alastair's lips and a glow in his eyes that told her plainly she had hit the right note. But it was only for that moment. For the most part, he was charming to the others, but seemed to be unable to bring himself to be charming to her. He watched her with a brooding expression. She was certain that he missed none of the exchanges between Vernon and herself, but she did not, on that account, lessen her affectionate attitude. It was natural for Vernon to stand with his arm about her, and she did not evade it. It was natural and customary for him to smile at her across the room with an intimate and loving smile; as natural for her to do the same. Vernon, who had sometimes felt that most of the loving was on his side, was reassured and content.

Then one afternoon the boys and three-year-old Jennifer came to show them a kitten which Jean-Pierre had brought up from the village for them.

'It's a marmalade kitten,' Jennifer explained, running after it to snatch it up every time it escaped her clutches. 'And it has blue eyes.'

Since they were having tea in the garden, they

invited the children to stay. Immediately afterwards the boys were off and away, leaving Jennifer behind, so that Cristina held out a hand to her and offered to take her back; and since the kitten constantly escaped Jennifer's rather frantic hold, Cristina took the kitten too.

They were in the passage of the house, looking for Marguerite, when Alastair came out of the study. Cristina thought he must have seen them approaching across the lawn.

'We were looking for Marguerite,' she explained.

'I believe Marguerite has a free afternoon. She's probably gone home to the village. Jennifer, run and find your mother. She's upstairs.'

Jennifer, taking the kitten from Cristina, trotted off, calling her mother.

'We wondered,' Cristina began, 'if you and Sylvana would like to come to dinner to-morrow evening. Vernon's sister Anne is arriving with a friend, Roger McIntyre, who says he knows you slightly.'

'McIntyre. Roger. Yes, he's the younger brother of my friend Archie McIntyre. But don't stand out here in the passage. Come in.'

He ushered Christina into his room, while she was protesting.

'No, no, I don't want to disturb you. I simply wanted to give you the dinner invitation. You can let us know when you've talked to Sylvana.'

'I think I may safely accept for both of us. The Walford family is altogether so delightful and friendly that Sylvana has really taken to them.'

'Good,' said Cristina. 'You wanted her to come out of her shell. But ask her anyway, and let us know.'

'I'll do that,' he said.

Cristina turned to leave, but his voice caused her to turn back.

'You are still living in your small apartment?' he asked her.

She was surprised by the question.

'No, as a matter of fact, I've given it up.'

'Where are you living, then—when you are in England?'

'At the moment I'm homeless,' she said with a smile. 'But all my bits and pieces are at the Walfords' house. I'm always sure of a welcome there.'

'That can't be as convenient for you, surely?'

'It's a temporary measure. I expect I shall get a bigger and better flat.'

'Yes, the other must have been rather cramped,' he agreed.

She was still surprised by the turn the conversation had taken.

'I was quite happy there when I couldn't afford anything better,' she said.

'*Are* you happy, Cristina?' he asked.

She was now slightly puzzled. Was he harking back now to what had transpired between themselves?

'What do you think?' she asked him. 'You know Vernon. You've seen us together. I've been aware of you watching us.'

'I'm sorry if it embarrassed you.'

'It didn't embarrass me, but I *have* wondered why you sometimes looked so disapproving.'

'I wasn't aware that I looked disapproving.'

'Well, you did. But why?'

He did not answer for a while, but continued to look at her from his dark eyes with the analytical and somewhat brooding expression she had noticed before.

'Why?' she asked him again.

'I have no right to look approving or disapproving. Your affairs are your own business.'

'Quite; but that sounds disapproving for a start. But I can't imagine what I've done to earn disapproval.'

'No?'

'No. My conscience is clear.'

'I'm delighted to hear it,' he said drily. 'Let us consider the conversation closed.'

'No, I'm damned if I will!' she exclaimed, suddenly angry. 'Not simply at your pleasure. You started this off by asking me if I was happy; implying that there might be some doubt of it. You go on to imply that I've done something that ought to lie on my conscience, and then you calmly tell me the conversation is closed. If you have something to complain about, come straight out with it. I hate beating about the bush.'

'Then, if I'm to come straight out with it, I must say that I very much disapprove—for you, Cristina, for *you*: other people may do what they like—of the way of life you've chosen.'

She looked completely blank. She gazed at him, not understanding. Then a perplexed frown appeared on her forehead.

'The way of life I've chosen,' she repeated. 'What way of life is that? No different from most people, as far as I can see.'

'Well, if most people live like that, though I should have thought they were still in the minority, I still don't like it for you. Not,' he added, 'that I have any rights in the matter at all. I have only opinions.'

'I don't understand a word you're saying,' she declared. 'I haven't chosen any way of life, yet.

Except, of course, that I'm going to share it with Vernon?'

'Or would it be truer to say that you *are* sharing it with Vernon?'

'At the moment, yes, because he's on holiday.'

'Not all the time? Not in London? Not in that little apartment of yours?'

She stared at him, and slowly the implication in his words became obvious to her; and to her great annoyance a slow blush spread across her cheeks and then receded to leave her quite pale. She looked at him with contempt.

'Like all "virtuous" people, you think the worst,' she said coldly.

'Isn't it true, that you're living together there?'

'Why should I answer your questions? As you said yourself, my affairs are my own business.'

'Cristina, tell me! Isn't it true?'

'I must say I'm surprised,' she said, watching him coldly, 'that you should jump to that sort of conclusion . . .' She broke off, the explanation for it suddenly dawning upon her. 'Oh,' she said, as the enlightenment continued. 'Oh yes, I do see. Of course.' She looked at him with a new awareness. 'Miss Usher,' she said, 'the charming Miss Usher.'

'Yes, it was Miss Usher,' he said. 'She apparently stumbled into a love nest.'

'And stirred up a hornet's nest,' said Cristina. 'So she came back here, knowing that her job here was finished and she had to leave the chateau, and told you that she had found Vernon and me living together. And you believed her.'

His dark eyes looked straight into hers.

'You only have to tell me it isn't true,' he said.

'I shouldn't have to tell you,' she said angrily.

' Let me tell you something else. Miss Usher had the same charming story to tell about you and Sylvana. Not for the first time. She told me in the spring that you were living together as man and wife. When she came to the apartment she told both Vernon and myself. And we didn't believe her! We recognised the spite in an embittered woman. But not you! You were quite prepared to believe it of me.'

' Cristina Just say it isn't true.'

' No, it has nothing to do with you.'

' Cristina.' He came towards her across the room but whatever he would have said or done was frustrated by the opening of the door, as Sylvana came into the study. He turned away at once, towards the window, but Cristina smiled frankly at Sylvana.

' I came over to ask you and Alastair to dinner tomorrow evening,' she said. ' Somebody who knows Alastair is coming with Anne Walford.'

' Somebody who knows Alastair?' queried Sylvana, and immediately said: ' Oh, I don't think we can tomorrow, but thank you.'

' I've already accepted,' said Alastair from the window.

Cristina thought that Sylvana looked quite harassed, and smiled reassuringly at her, thinking she had a recurrence of her shyness.

' You'll like them, Sylvana,' she said. ' They're both so nice. Anne is Vernon's sister and Roger is her present young man.'

' Oh,' said Sylvana. ' Yes, I'm sorry to be so stupid. I was mistaking the date. Yes, we shall love to come to dinner tomorrow.'

' Fine. Quarter to eight? Good. Well, I must go back now. We'll see you tomorrow.'

She made for the door and Sylvana accompanied her.

'I came down to thank you for bringing Jenny back. We're so afraid the children are bothering you. They're so delighted to have so much going on, we can't keep them away from your house.'

Cristina reassured her, and succeeded in making her escape while doing so; but as she walked back across the velvety lawn, conflicting emotions filled her mind. Anger chiefly, that he should have been so ready to believe Miss Usher's scandal.

It did not surprise her at all that Miss Usher had gone out of her way to give him a wrong impression. She was filled with vindictiveness and spite because she had to leave the chateau; but surely any reasonable woman would know that her job would cease on the death of her employer. And she had, after all, had a pleasant job with a great many advantages, including the rent of her own cottage while she was living here with Grandmother in considerable comfort, a legacy of five thousand pounds, and some valuable jewellery which might or might not be legally hers. Cristina did not for one moment believe that her grandmother ever said she would leave the chateau to Miss Usher, or even entertained the idea. Grandmother had too good a sense of what was suitable in the family to do such a thing. She had made a will, and if she had intended to alter it, she would have done so. No, that was a badly aimed shot in the dark that meant nothing. But Miss Usher would quite happily malign Cristina, who had inherited what she envied so much.

She had also tried to give Cristina and Vernon the same impression about Alastair and Sylvana. It occurred to Cristina at that point that Alastair had not denied it, though he had been so anxious that Cristina should. Was it possible that what was sauce for the goose was not sauce for the gander? She did not know what to believe, but felt inclined to think that this was but another of Miss Usher's troublemaking scandals.

Anne and Roger arrived on the following day and the house was full of talk and comings-and-goings and cheerful occasions such as mid-morning coffee out on the terrace and lazing interminably over after-luncheon coffee in the tower room.

'And there's a dinner party this evening,' Cristina told Anne. 'The Buchanans are coming over.'

'Good. We love parties.'

'So do we. We had to smooth Louise down, for she wondered how many more people would be arriving. But now one of her daughters is helping in the kitchen, and earning money, and they're chattering away in the kitchen, thoroughly enjoying themselves.'

'I expect our doings are reported all over the village,' said Vernon.

'Well, as nothing's going on that we have to be ashamed of, I don't particularly mind that,' said Cristina.

'Is it a dressing-up party?' asked Anne. 'Or dressing down?'

'I think dress-up, don't you? It makes it more of an occasion.'

Roger, who had been on a tour of the house and grounds before lunch, now said:

'Two things you need, Cristina, to make this place ideal. A swimming pool, preferably heated, and a tennis court.'

'Yes, that would be marvellous, if one intended to stay; but I'm afraid it's going to be sold.'

'Isn't that too bad?' said Anne, smiling. 'How can she bear to sell what would be such a nice holiday house for *us*?'

'I can hardly bear it,' said Cristina. 'I'm getting so fond of it.' She turned to Vernon. 'I can understand poor Usher hating to leave it. So it had better be sold before we all get too attached to it.'

'Why sell it at all when you like it so much?' asked Roger.

'Because it's impractical when Vernon and I have to live near his work. Oh, we've gone into it lots of times, but there was no reason why we shouldn't enjoy it for *this* summer.'

The family split up for the afternoon, Mrs Walford and Cristina making splendid flower arrangements for the house, but in the evening they all gathered in the tower room to await their guests. Cristina and Vernon were down first.

'What a perfectly beautiful hostess,' Vernon said, standing still to admire her. She was wearing a yellow dress that glinted with lines of gold as she moved, gold sandals and heavy old-fashioned gold jewellery that had been her grandmother's. When he would have kissed her, she held him off with both hands extended.

'Don't you dare to spoil my hair or my make-up or any of this carefully prepared Me,' she said, smiling.

'Then I kiss your hand, *mademoiselle*,' he said, and did so.

'You have to be host for me, Vernon. Drinks and things.'

'Of course. I bet you never saw yourself, Cristie love, as the *doyenne* of a French chateau giving splendid dinner parties.'

'*Jamais de ma vie*,' she said. 'Never in my life.

But it's rather fun while it lasts. Oh, here's your mother. Mrs Walford, you look lovely.'

It was the first compliment of many, for Anne in a gorgeous sari, and Flora in lilac, had also made loving preparations for the party. The men were less formal and had settled for light-weight suits, but made up for it, as Anne commented, by a flower-garden of beautiful coloured shirts. And it was with some curiosity that they waited for Alastair and Sylvana. Cristina wondered if she should have told them about dressing. It might embarrass them if they came in ordinary day clothes to find this resplendent party waiting for them.

She need not have worried. Alastair, as usual, looked distinguished. His height and build allowed him to carry all his clothes with a rare elegance. Sylvana, immaculate as ever, wore a trouser suit of gold. Her smooth dark hair was pulled back as usual into a knot at the back, and the olive oval of her face was delicately made up. She wore topaz jewellery, huge topaz earrings at her ears. How did she manage always to look as if the couturier, the hairdresser and the beautician had just this moment finished with her? She certainly made an impact when she entered, and she seemed to search first of all for the strangers in their midst. She was introduced and seemed relieved to find them harmless.

Almost at the start, Cristina realised that she need not worry about this party. It went with a swing. Anne said in her usual forthright way that they all looked like a coloured advertisement for something terribly expensive and useless. Vernon and his father carried the drinks, and the others were soon absorbed in conversations in various parts of the room.

Roger McIntyre and Anne were talking to Alastair and Sylvana, and after Alastair's enquiries about his friend Archie, and an exchange of news, the talk turned to the chateau itself.

'I understand your house is also inside the castle walls,' Roger said to Alastair.

'Yes. The chateau was a ruin when somebody bought it to restore it; but the owners had built our house, rather provincial French, I'm afraid, among the ruins about sixty years ago. Cristina's grandmother was much more interested in building a new house, incorporating this beautiful old tower room and part of the old walls. And a beautiful job she made of it, too.'

'She did, indeed.' They all admired the tower room.

'Great pity that it's going to be sold again,' said Roger.

Alastair looked at him enquiringly.

'So Cristina said this afternoon,' Roger went on. 'She says it's too impractical when she and Vernon have to live near his work. I suppose she's right, but it does seem a pity to part with it.'

Mr Walford joined their group.

'Your glass is empty, Mr Buchanan,' he said. 'Let me bring you another. And for you, Roger?'

'Let me come and help you, sir,' said Roger, politely; and the two men moved away, and Anne quite changed the subject by saying to Alastair:

'You've quite made Flora's holiday for her, Mr Buchanan . . .'

'Alastair,' he interrupted her. 'Let's not be too formal.'

'Well, you've made Flora's holiday for her, Alastair, by making her free of your stables. She adores the boys, too.'

'I think they adore her. She's been very kind, riding with them.'

'When are you going to start Jennifer?'

'Not yet,' interposed Sylvana at once. 'She's much too young.'

'Yes, we can give her a little time,' said Alastair.

'I don't think she likes horses, Alastair,' Sylvana went on. 'You know she is a little nervous. I don't want her to run the slightest risk.'

If Cristina had been there, she would have been surprised at even so much of a protest from the usually silent Sylvana; but Anne simply realised that the child's mother was nervous on her account, and would probably communicate her nervousness to the child, and however much she might encourage her sons to ride, she was going to discourage it for the young Jennifer.

The whole party moved into the dining room in an irregular straggle, seating themselves according to the place cards. Cristina had insisted upon Mr and Mrs Walford taking the head and foot of the table. The food was good, the wine and the conversation flowed, and at the end of the meal, Alastair surprised Cristina very much by rising and proposing a toast to her, for making this delightful occasion possible. 'I don't think this chateau has enjoyed such a lively party or such stimulating conversation for a long time,' he said. And Cristina, refusing to reply formally, smiled at him across the table and said: 'Well, let's hope it won't be the last such occasion.'

'Sylvana and I hope not,' he said.

He entertained them all in return: not at his house, but at Madame Delavent's small restaurant in the village. For this occasion, their long table occupied nearly half of the restaurant. Detailed discussion of the menu had gone on beforehand, the flowers had been sent from the chateau gardens and arranged by Marguerite, and the table linen had obviously come from the same source.

There were continual other exchanges: the children taken out by the Walford party, various members of that family riding the Buchanan horses, a fairly frequent exchange of drinks before luncheon or dinner. The two people who did not come together were Cristina and Alastair; but Cristina could not decide whether this was chance or a deliberate act on Alastair's part. So that when he asked her one day if she could spare him a few moments to discuss the house, she was surprised.

'We shall all be out until the early evening,' she said. 'We're going to see the famous gorge. But before or after dinner would be fine. Will you come over?'

'Perhaps you would come to us, as you are rather crowded at the moment. Leave it until after dinner—you may be in need of a little relaxation after walking all afternoon through the gorge.'

So it was arranged, and Cristina gave the matter no more thought, having become accustomed to this formal Alastair and expecting the formality to remain. Their party drove to the gorge in two cars, admiring the great clefts, peering down into the water-worn depths, fascinated by the boulders and great rocks worn over hundreds of years into smooth and intriguing shapes by the swirl and the rush of the waters. They came back to the chateau in the early evening, pleased, as Alastair had suggested, to relax in the restfulness of the tower room, talking pleasantly over a leisurely drink before dinner.

After dinner, Cristina excused herself and went across the darkened lawns towards the lights of the

127

other house where she was admitted by Alastair himself. As he had suggested 'perhaps you would come to us', Cristina had supposed that Sylvana, too, would be there; but once again she was in bed with a bad headache. Briefly, Cristina wondered if this headache was a fabrication of Alastair's, and then remembered that it was Miss Usher who had thrown doubt on Sylvana's headaches. And since Miss Usher had proved so unreliable on other occasions, why should she be believed on this one?

'I hope she'll soon be better,' Cristina said. 'She has so many headaches. Couldn't something be done about it?'

'I'm quite sure they're nervous headaches,' Alastair said. 'The moment she's worried about anything, they seem to recur.'

'And is she worried at the moment?'

'I think she's a little worried about the fate of the house, although she hasn't admitted it. But the moment she realised it was going to be sold, I think she began to worry in case we had to go back to England. And this, of course, is what I wanted to discuss with you.'

'The fate of the house?'

'Yes. When we were speaking to Roger at your party the other night, he said that you had decided to sell. Sylvana heard it. So, being very much concerned as your tenant, I wondered if you could tell me more about it. You know I'm interested in keeping the tenancy here.'

'But Roger was mistaken in speaking so definitely. I haven't absolutely decided to sell, although of course it does seem to be the only practical thing.'

'Then I beg your pardon. I seem to have

brought you over on false pretences, but he certainly did speak definitely. So things haven't changed? They are just as they were before?'

'Yes. I seem to be dithering, I expect, but I can, after all, sell at any time, and it did seem a good idea to enjoy it during the summer; as we're most certainly enjoying it.'

'An enjoyment that has spread out to include this house and family, for which we are all indebted to you. But you will do me the favour of letting me know when you do decide anything, as we're rather closely involved?'

'Yes, I promise you that.'

'Then at the moment we have nothing to discuss. I apologise for disturbing your evening. I expect you would like to hurry back to your guests.'

'No, I hope I haven't appeared anxious to. They're all quite happy.'

'Then have some coffee and a liqueur with me, Cristina.'

'Lovely, I'd like to.'

For a few moments she had felt a strange sympathy for him. It occurred to her that he might not be living at all a life of his own choosing; staying here because of Sylvana's whims or her strange temperament; dining alone because the children were long since in bed and Sylvana with one more of her migraine headaches. In her own house, the Walfords and Roger filled the place with life, always full of plans and conversation. It struck her that this was a quiet house. So she sat and waited contentedly for the coffee to arrive, and watched Alastair pouring the cognac and bringing a glass to her side.

'Have you and Vernon plans for where you will live in England?' he asked her, when the coffee had arrived and he had poured it into two small cups.

'Out of London, we hope. South, I imagine, fairly near his family. We like Sussex, so perhaps it will be Surrey-Sussex borders.'

'Beautiful country,' he agreed. 'And very cosy.' She smiled at him.

'Not like Sutherland, certainly,' she said.

'No. You have no idea how wild it can be in Sutherland. But I like a wild beauty.'

'And must be looking forward to that glorious twelfth.'

'Indeed,' he agreed. 'Indeed.' And once more she felt that he would like to be away from this place, up on his lonely moors, fishing the lakes and rivers, climbing the mountains, feeling once more the mountain air on his face, the scree beneath his boots.

'We went to the gorge this afternoon,' she said. 'It was wild enough there. A fantastic place. I think there's still plenty of wild country left in France.'

At last she said she must go; and he said politely he would see her to her door.

'Oh no, it's quite unnecessary,' she said.

'Yes, I'm sure it is, but I'll do it all the same.'

They went out of the house into the darkened garden, and halfway across the wide sweeping lawn, he detained her with a hand on her arm.

'See how gay it looks at the moment,' he said, and she stopped and looked towards the two houses, some distance apart, backed by the old chateau walls. Both houses were lit up, golden light shining from several windows, reassuring against the surrounding blackness. 'And how dark it will be at the Chateau de la Falaise when you are gone again,' he said.

She did not reply, but began to walk on again.

'Yes,' she said at last. 'It will be quiet for the children.'

There was a pause before he said quietly:

'I wasn't really thinking of the children.'

She stood still once more, in no hurry to return to her house party. She felt that she could stay in this darkened garden contentedly for a long time. She said:

'Let's have a little walk. It's so lovely in the warm night.'

They turned together, taking a different direction, came to the narrow door in the castle wall and went through into the formal garden, pacing the paths slowly, coming through the deeper darkness of the tall boundary trees to the spot where they had once admired the moonlit village together. But there was no moon to-night and even the light of the stars was obscured by cloud. It was very still, very quiet and very dark.

At last Cristina said in a voice little louder than a whisper:

'I don't *have* to go back when the others go. There's nothing urgent calling me back to England. I've given up my flat. Vernon has to go because of his work, and the others too. But I could stay a little longer.'

She was speaking so quietly that she might almost have been thinking her thoughts privately, but Alastair turned to her at once.

'Then stay, Cristina.'

She paused, taking a long breath, balanced on the edge of making a decision.

'Yes. All right,' she said at last.

He took her hand, holding it in his own. Her fingers turned in his to clasp them. They went into each other's arms as naturally, as comfortably, as blissfully, as if this was their predestined home. They clung together, wordlessly, almost motionlessly, the sheer relief of being together again forcing out all thought. His arms were so strong and close about her that she relaxed completely, feeling she would fall if he let her go; and when she sighed a long sigh of happiness, he leaned his head down to her and kissed her.

She had no idea how long it lasted. She had abandoned all idea of time when she abandoned all restraint. She gave herself up to that kiss so completely and utterly that even Alastair was surprised, taking in delight and rapture what she gave so freely.

'Cristina, I love you,' he said.

'Don't say that,' she groaned. 'Don't say that.'

'I love you. It's true. And irrevocable. Since the very first.'

She shook her head, refusing to acknowledge his love, but still kissed him with the same ardour when he kissed her again.

They stood together, arms about each other, straining together, swaying slightly with the intensity of their emotion.

'What are we going to do?' he asked her quietly.

'Nothing, nothing, nothing. What *can* we do?'

'God knows, but if you, Cristina, feel the way I feel . . .' He broke off, because he wanted her to say what she felt, but she could not; and would not if she had known definitely, because too much was at stake here.

'I can't think,' she whispered. 'I can't think.'

'No,' he reassured her, and simply held her in his arms, but feeling already the stirring of passion that would want to make her entirely his.

After a long time she moved to extricate herself from his embrace.

'Don't move,' he whispered.

'Yes, I have to.' She put her hands on his arms and pushed them away. 'I have to think. This sort of thing can't go on.'

'I love you, Cristina.'

'But if it's true, it's a tragedy,' she cried.

'Hush,' he said; and in that one word they both realised what had happened. They had entered into an illicit relationship. They had to take care. That one word 'hush' meant that they must not be overheard, must not be overlooked, or discovered.

'This is all wrong,' she said. 'We have to stop it.'

'If we can,' he said soberly, and suddenly they were clinging together again, because neither of them wanted to stop it. They wanted to be together, closely together, and felt it pain to drag themselves apart again.

'This is love, Cristina,' he said to her softly. 'You love me, too.'

'No, no,' she protested. 'I love Vernon. This must be an evil kind of magic. An evil spell. Oh, God, I hope I see sense in the morning.'

'Yes, you will see sense in the morning. And I shall see sense, too. And we shall know that nothing can be done. So are we to have nothing at all, Cristina?'

'Nothing at all,' she said seriously, and it seemed like an amputation, cutting off all delight, all rapture.

'But every time we see each other alone, this is what we shall want. I know it and you know it.'

'Then we mustn't see each other alone.'

'But when the others go back to England?'

'I'd better go back with them, Alastair.'

'Stay a little,' he persuaded softly. 'Just a little while. I can't lose you so suddenly, so completely. Let us have *something* to remember.'

'That would be madness. But, Alastair, I *want* to stay so much.'

At that admission he took her back into his arms once more, kissed her once more, before she drew away again.

'I must go. Somebody will come to look for me soon.'

'They think you are in my house. They won't intrude.'

'No. I'm determined I must go.'

So they walked back together, hand clasping hand; and just before they came into view of Cristina's front door round the tower, he raised her hand to his lips and kissed it.

'Cristina, I'm sorry I ever doubted you.'

'It doesn't matter now,' she said.

'Good-night, *mon coeur*. Remember that I love you.'

He left her there, but Cristina could not immediately return to the lively company she would find in the tower room. She paced slowly along the edge of the grass, trying to recover her poise, trying to bring herself down to earth after the strange, exalted region she had been in with Alastair.

She felt a sense of loss at being parted from him, at being loosed from his arms, and she asked herself why there should be this intensity of feeling when she had parted so many times from Vernon without feeling it. Was it because she knew that she and Vernon would be happily reunited soon, whereas with Alastair there was no possibility of happy union? But she knew she had never shared such an intensity with Vernon, not even in the days of the first kisses, the first realisation that theirs was a deep and abiding relationship; that they meant more to each other than anybody else had meant to them before. There had never been this particular delight, this unspoiled rapture, this flowing together. Was it love? she asked herself. If so, it could only be put away from them, for there were too many lives concerned that could only be destroyed. Vernon she thought of with a great surge of affection. She could do nothing to hurt him. And what of Sylvana, the so-nervous Sylvana who needed somebody to lean on, somebody to care for her? What of the three children?

She made her way into the house. She had not to wait for the morning to see sense. She was seeing already the only possible course before her. She knew what she *must* do, but what she wanted to do was to go straight back to Alastair to feel the utter comfort of his arms about her again.

CHAPTER VII

The following morning, Roger and Anne took Mr
and Mrs Walford on an expedition to two cathedrals
in different cities which they were interested to see.
They intended to be away for lunch and return
some time in the afternoon. Vernon and Flora
were going to ride, but only if they were sure they
were not depriving Alastair himself.

'Walk over to the stables with us, darling,' Vernon said to Cristina.

'Oh, I think I'd better talk to Louise about
lunch,' she said.

'You can do that afterwards. Come along.'

She went along with them, and they found the
two boys there and Jean-Pierre saddling the ponies.
Angus and Neil were hoping to be invited to ride
with them, and they were not disappointed.

'But you must go to the house first,' Vernon insisted, 'to see if your Uncle Alastair intends to
ride.'

'I don't think he does,' said Angus.

'You go and find out. We're always borrowing
his horses.'

Angus went to find out and Jean-Pierre began
saddling Firebrand. When Angus reappeared,
Alastair was with him.

'Good morning,' called Vernon when they were
still some distance away. 'We didn't mean to
disturb you, but we did want to be sure you weren't
riding yourself.'

'No, I'm not riding, thanks. Are you sure you
want the boys with you? They can ride on the
plateau alone.'

'They're very welcome. It's we who are very much in your debt.'

Alastair and Cristina watched as the horses were made ready and the riders mounted. They avoided looking at each other. They accompanied the riders as they clattered across the stable yard and went between the solid stone piers of the stable yard gate, and watched as they set off across the plateau. Then they turned back together, and Cristina was grateful for the presence of Jean-Pierre in the stables. Yet, even as she remembered him, he came out of one of the outhouses, mounted on the lawnmower, making for the sweeping lawn between the houses.

Cristina would have followed him to make her escape, but as they passed the stables, Alastair took her hand and pulled her roughly into the stables with him.

'Were you going without a word to me?' he asked, and his voice was also ragged and rough, and she looked at him and forgave him for the roughness. She took her hand from his and they looked at each other in the dusty gloom with the hay and horse smell of the stables around them. His eyes were dark and fathomless. Hers were clear and held an appeal in them. An appeal that he would not touch her? or that he would?

'Did you sleep?' he asked her.

'Yes. After a time. Did you?'

'No, hardly at all. I was awake, thinking of you.'

She shook her head at him.

'Not very profitable thoughts,' she said.

'No. But one thing I'm sure of, Cristina. You and I should marry.'

'No!' she exclaimed sharply. 'It's impossible.'

' I didn't say it was possible. I said it's what we *should* do.'

' But can't.'

' I love you. And I believe you love me. What a life we could have together! I love your freshness and your candour. But my hands are tied.'

' I know. I'm tied, too.'

He held his arms open to her and she could not resist going into them, to be drawn closer and tighter; but now she felt the sting of tears behind her eyes, for now there was something of resignation in their attitude. He had admitted his responsibilities, he had said his hands were tied; and she should have been glad of it, yet she wanted to weep. She flung her arms round his neck, holding herself yet closer to him, and they kissed with a rapture that was beginning to hold despair.

When at last they parted, they walked to the open door, to the brilliant sunlight of the outside.

' There's nothing I can do,' he said. ' Much as I love you, I can't desert Sylvana.'

' You don't seem to think of Vernon at all,' she said.

' I do, but Vernon is a complete person, self-assured, self-reliant. He would always be able to look after himself, even if he lost you. Sylvana couldn't. She is dependent, she has a family to care for, she has already lost Angus. How can I leave her?'

' Alastair, it sounds as if you don't love her!'

' I love *you*. I'm very fond of Sylvana. I've always been fond of her.'

' Is that enough for you to propose marriage?'

There was a silence as they began to walk back slowly towards the house. Then he said:

' I didn't propose marriage, Cristina. Sylvana

did.'

She looked quickly at him, in surprise.

'And there was nobody else I loved. That isn't a sufficient reason, I know. I would like you to understand the real situation, Cristina . . .'.

Whatever the real situation was, Cristina was not to discover that morning, for Marguerite appeared from Alastair's house, calling his name and beckoning to him, letting him know that London wanted him on the telephone.

'Damn the telephone,' he said softly.

'You must go,' Cristina said, 'and I have to go and talk to Louise. *Au 'voir*, Alastair.'

'*Au 'voir*, my love.'

Cristina walked back to her own house. She talked to Louise in the kitchen about lunch and dinner, and then went into the tower room. She had probably a couple of hours to herself, but she did not need so long to decide what was the wisest and most sensible thing to do. She and Alastair must keep apart. This would not be too difficult while the Walfords were still here, but would be almost impossible afterwards. Vernon himself had to leave at the end of the week, Anne and Roger a few days later. And a week after that, the Walford parents and Flora would go away; and the obviously sensible solution was for Cristina to go with them.

She had told Alastair that she would stay for a while, but that was before the wild eruption of feeling between them. Now it was obvious that they would never meet in privacy without the desperate urge to fall into each other's arms. No, she would have to return with the others, and Alastair would surely see the sense of her decision.

It was all very well to be sensible, she told herself in the days that followed, but common sense was a poor consolation for the longings that assailed her. Knowing that he was there, such a short distance away, harried her continually. She thought up excuses for visiting him, knowing that she would not go, however good the excuses. She seized every opportunity of getting away from the chateau, trying to free herself from the ambience that included Alastair; and this meant that she and Vernon were often out in the car together, exploring the countryside, or on the river together, drifting lazily with the current, or Vernon rowing in a leisurely fashion while Cristina tried to immerse herself in the calm, peaceful, reassuring atmosphere. She tried not to admit to herself that, after being with Alastair, it was like being with a much-loved brother to be with Vernon.

The others in the house teased them a little about their desire to be off alone.

'They're in love, poor things,' said Flora, who being at the moment in love only with horses, could afford to scoff.

'Well, Vernon has to go at the end of the week,' pointed out his mother.

'What a pity,' said Cristina, wishing he could stay longer.

'What a pity,' he agreed, 'but I have to earn a living, love. It's a pity we can't have holidays whenever we want them, but I've already had three of my four weeks this year.'

'We can't all be Alastair Buchanans,' added his father. 'He apparently sits in his study, manipulating finance in what must be a very intricate brain, telephones London almost every day and visits it occasionally. That must leave him about three-quarters of the year to do just as he likes.'

'The brainy bit sounds as dry as dust,' declared

the outdoor Flora.

'He has an antidote to that in the gardens of the chateau,' said Vernon.

'Which he does keep most beautifully,' put in Mrs Walford. 'I seldom walk in the garden without discovering him pruning or training or doing something equally useful.'

'Still, it doesn't suit him,' declared Anne. 'You'd expect him to be doing much more exciting things. It's a strange sort of secluded life they live here, isn't it?'

'Some people actually like to be quiet and secluded,' her father said with a smile; for that was the kind of life he also liked.

Cristina thought that Alastair did like quiet and seclusion at times, but it was not the seclusion of the Chateau de la Falaise. He liked the wild beauty of Sutherland with its gales and its tempests, its mountains and its deserted bays, its cliffs and rivers and lakes. Was he to be for ever deprived of them if he married Sylvana, or might they effect a compromise by which he could sometimes have the two boys there with him? She knew that she herself would love that countryside. Especially with Alastair, she acknowledged to herself, to show her everything that he loved, to walk with him over the mountains; and to have the best of both worlds by coming to London with him whenever business demanded. But that was a dream, and dreaming was a weakness to be discouraged.

At the end of the week Vernon left, consoling himself with the thought that Cristina would not be long after him. Then Anne and Roger departed, and the house would have been much quieter but for the unexpected arrival of two of Cristina's friends, who, driving through France,

141

had found themselves in her vicinity. They stayed for three nights, and when they too were gone, the remaining four people in the house began to look towards their own departure.

'Shall we ask the Buchanans for a last dinner party, Cristina?' asked Mrs Walford. 'They've been so very kind to us while we've been here. My family has practically taken over their horses and stables.'

'Yes, let's do that,' agreed Cristina, who was beginning to count the days, and even the hours, remaining to her: not with any pleasurable feeling of anticipation, but with regret at their passing.

So Sylvana and Alastair arrived once more for dinner, gathering with the Walfords and Cristina in the beautiful circular room of the tower for drinks beforehand. Alastair seemed quiet and withdrawn, but Sylvana, who seemed at last to feel safe with these people, was smiling and almost talkative.

'I'm so sorry you're leaving,' she said. 'We are all going to miss you so much, and the children will be quite desolate.'

'Ah, needs must,' said Mr Walford, smiling back at her. 'We would like to stay, but duty calls.'

'Duty doesn't call *me*,' protested Flora. 'I have long school holidays.'

'But you also have a visit to make to the Gregsons,' her mother reminded her.

'Oh, the Gregsons.' Flora dismissed them with a contemptuous wave of the hand.

'You know you wouldn't miss that. They also have horses.'

'But does duty call Cristina?' asked Sylvana. 'I had an idea of asking her to come to Paris with me.' Cristina looked up quickly, and was aware that

Alastair, across the room, also glanced at Sylvana with so much surprise that Cristina knew immediately that he was no part of this plan.

'Paris?' she queried. 'I didn't know you were going to Paris, Sylvana.'

'Yes. Alastair has business there and I need to buy clothes. I thought it might be nice for us to be in Paris together, Cristina.'

This was cause for further surprise, for it was the first overture of friendship that Sylvana had made.

'You aren't working any more,' Sylvana reminded her, 'and I think you said you've given up your apartment. You could come to Paris.'

'I must admit that it's rather a nice idea,' Cristina told her, realising that the proximity to Alastair was her main reason for thinking so. 'But I've been invited to stay with Mrs Walford.'

'Oh, we shall still be at home when you've had your trip to Paris,' Mrs Walford assured her.

'And Vernon expects me,' protested Cristina.

'Vernon, too, will still be there,' smiled Mrs Walford. 'You go off with Sylvana and buy some pretty clothes in Paris.' She reflected that Cristina, who had had to be economical in the past, could do with new clothes from Paris more than Sylvana, who seemed to have an endless variety.

Cristina glanced at Alastair, but he remained silent, neither encouraging nor discouraging this plan. She said:

'Let me think about it, Sylvana. But it does sound rather fun.'

They went in to dinner, and it seemed to be assumed by the Walfords that Cristina would go to Paris and that they would return to England without her. It was more their decision than Cristina's that left her behind at the chateau when their car was finally loaded and Cristina walked to the wide gates to open them.

It was very quiet in Cristina's house when they had gone. Louise's daughter was no longer needed in the kitchen, and Louise herself left after lunch, usually driven down to the village by Cristina. Sylvana, with her newly acquired confidence in Cristina, insisted that she should walk across the intervening lawns in the evening to have dinner with herself and Alastair. It was painful for Cristina to be in the same room as Alastair and scarcely dare to look into his eyes; more painful still not to be with him. She told herself she should have refused the invitation to Paris and returned to England with the Walfords, for nothing but additional heartache could be derived from this trip.

Three-year-old Jennifer made a great fuss at the last minute, saying, when her mother kissed her goodbye: 'I want to go to Paris, I want to go to Paris,' over and over again, becoming more tearful every moment, until Alastair told Marguerite to take the children inside. Rather tearful herself, Sylvana said:

'I always tell her when I'm going away, and when I'm coming back, but I do hate leaving her. And the boys, of course, but they are older and more sensible.'

In Paris, their hotel rooms were booked. Three single rooms, Cristina noticed, each with its luxurious bathroom, each with a balcony overlooking the lovely heart of Paris. Alastair and Sylvana came to knock on her door before dinner, to take her down for an aperitif.

'But I have to remind you both,' he said, as they sat in comfort with their drinks, 'that I *am* here

144

on business. So you must entertain yourselves during the day.'

'That's why it's so nice to have Cristina here,' Sylvana told him. 'We intend to have a wonderful time.'

The visit certainly started out that way. They breakfasted together each morning, and then separated, Alastair on his business pursuits, Cristina and Sylvana on a leisurely tour of exclusive and certainly expensive boutiques. Cristina, who had often shopped in a great rush in her lunch time, admired Sylvana's leisurely progress, for Sylvana would stop for coffee here, for an aperitif there, often simply because she wanted to sit at the pavement cafés and see the world go by. In several of the boutiques she was a valued client; and Cristina found herself being seated comfortably by Sylvana's side, while dresses, coats, trouser suits and evening wear were brought out for their approval. She thought that, without Sylvana, she would not have rated this individual attention. It was Sylvana's clothes, her elegance, her real jewellery, that earned so much politeness, so much eager desire to serve. Cristina wondered why she needed so many clothes when she refused to lead a social life; why her hair needed a hairdresser so often. Was it all for Alastair's benefit that she made herself so coolly perfect?

Cristina also bought some clothes, but with more caution. She could not forget her previous need for economy, could not approve of Paris prices and the spending of so much money on her personal adornment. She was convinced that she could look quite as elegant, as chic, without so much expenditure.

So three days passed. Early each evening, before

they all met downstairs for the aperitif, Sylvana telephoned the chateau to speak to the children. Each evening she was assured by Marguerite that all was well, the children were all happy, there were no temperatures, and so on. Only then could she join Alastair and Cristina and recount the story of her day for Alastair's benefit.

'So you are quite happy to stay longer?' Alastair asked.

'A day or two, I think,' she said. 'Not more.'

Yet the very next day changed her mind.

She had been buying gloves and silk squares, and trifles to take home for the children. They had lunched in a restaurant, Sylvana then declared they would have their coffee in the Champs Elysées, and had commandeered a taxi to take them there, where they had a table set some distance back from the road. Their coffee was ordered and they sat back to watch the passing scene. And it was then that Sylvana surprised Cristina by pushing her chair back with sudden force, rising to her feet, turning her back on the passing people and saying urgently, almost in panic:

'We must go. We must go back to the hotel at once!'

She was gathering up her small parcels and her bag. She walked quickly into the restaurant behind the open-air tables. Cristina, greatly astonished, followed her, detaining her inside with a touch on her arm.

'What's the matter, Sylvana? Aren't you well?'

She certainly did not look well. Every vestige of colour had deserted her olive cheeks, leaving her curiously pale and haggard; and her eyes were quite tormented.

'We must go back at once,' she repeated, hardly

seeming to know who Cristina was. 'I must find Alastair. We must go back.'

'All right. Wait here a moment. I'll get a taxi.' Cristina hurried out again, but it was the doorman who got a taxi for her; and she helped Sylvana into it, got in beside her and directed the driver to the hotel.

Sylvana hurried in as if to escape from something or somebody. Cristina paid for the taxi and again followed her. They went up in the lift together and into Sylvana's room. Sylvana flung everything she was carrying on to the bed, and began to walk up and down in a distracted fashion.

'Sylvana, what is it? Are you ill? Shall I call a doctor?'

'No, no, I'm not ill, I don't want a doctor. I want Alastair. We must go home at once. We must go to the chateau. Oh, *mon Dieu, mon Dieu!* Cristina, please see if Alastair is in the hotel.'

'You know he was going out of town to-day, Sylvana.'

'Oh, why must he be out of town when I need him? Please ring up the chateau and find out if the children are all right.'

'You know they are all right, you spoke to them yesterday evening. What is it? Have you had a premonition or something?'

'No, no. Oh dear, what shall I do? What shall I do?'

'Well, if you'd tell me what the matter is, I might be able to help you.'

'No, you can't help me. Nobody can help me. Nobody. Perhaps Alastair. Oh, I wish he were here, he would tell me what to do. We must go back to the chateau at once. Cristina, you could drive me back.'

'There's nothing so urgent that it can't wait for Alastair's return,' said Cristina as serenely and consolingly as she could, knowing that she would never dare to drive Alastair's Rolls-Royce away from Paris. 'You're not ill?'

'No.'

'And the children are all right. Then you've nothing to worry about. I'm going to order coffee and brandies for us both. You shouldn't alarm me in this fashion, Sylvana.'

She thought this would bring an apology from Sylvana, but Sylvana scarcely seemed to notice what Cristina had said. She was in a state of great mental agitation, and Cristina wondered what could possibly have induced this *crise de nerfs.* Was this an habitual state of affairs? Was this something that Alastair often had to endure?

She ordered the coffee and brandy, and waited until Sylvana had finished hers.

'Do you want me to stay with you?' she asked gently. 'Or would you rather be alone?'

'Would you stay? But I think I must go to bed. I have a sharp attack of migraine coming on.'

'Yes, I'll stay. I'll just go and get a book from my room.'

Cristina fetched her book, and when she returned Sylvana was in bed, the curtains partly drawn, her head buried in the pillow. Cristina went and sat by the window, reading; glancing from time to time at the motionless young woman in the bed. A real enigma, she decided. She had had no idea that Sylvana was so unstable. No wonder Alastair felt that he could never leave her to fend for herself.

It seemed an interminable afternoon. Cristina ordered tea to be sent up during the course of it, and Sylvana sipped hers, taking more migraine tablets, and still refusing to tell Cristina what her trouble was. At last, at the time for their evening aperitif, Alastair returned, and not finding them waiting for him downstairs, tapped gently on Sylvana's door.

Sylvana started up, looking, Cristina thought, quite frightened; and only sank back reassured when she saw it was Alastair on the threshold.

'Why, what's this?' asked Alastair gently. 'Aren't you well, Sylvana?'

'Migraine,' she said, dismissing it. 'Alastair, I want to go home immediately.'

'Home?' he queried. 'Where is home?'

'The chateau, of course. I want to go at once. Could we start immediately?'

'No, we could not,' he said, but still gently, still watching her. 'Why do you suddenly want to go?'

'I want to see the children, I want to be sure they are all right. I hate this place, I want to get away from Paris.'

'But you've been enjoying Paris. You said so.'

'No longer,' she said impatiently. 'Alastair, do take me home.'

'Now listen, Sylvana.' He went to the side of the bed, sat on the edge of it and took her hands into his. He looked across the room at Cristina. 'Do *you* know why this sudden change of heart, Cristina?' he asked.

'I have no idea, and Sylvana won't tell me. She had a sudden sort of *crise de nerfs* while we were having coffee in the Champs Elysées, and demanded to be brought back to the hotel. She certainly didn't *look* well.'

Alastair turned back to Sylvana.

'If you have a bad migraine, you don't want to travel to-night. You'll stay in bed and rest. And

149

I have had a long and busy day, and intend to enjoy my dinner to-night. But my business is finished now, so if you're so eager to return to the chateau, we'll leave first thing in the morning.'

'Oh, how can you think about dinner when I'm so worried?' she cried.

'Tell me what's worrying you,' he said gently, holding her hands closely in his own.

'I can't, I have such a bad headache,' she said. But his touch seemed to calm her. Cristina went to the door, to leave them alone together, and Alastair turned his head towards her.

'Downstairs in half an hour?' he queried. 'You and I need a drink and our dinner, even if Sylvana refuses.'

'Are you sure?' asked Cristina, distressed on Sylvana's account. Had Sylvana, by some strange means Cristina could not imagine, discovered the truth about Alastair and herself? It seemed impossible, but there seemed to be no other likely explanation for her sudden breakdown.

'Yes, I'm sure,' Alastair said, and Cristina went away to change for dinner, feeling more disturbed on Sylvana's account than she ever had before.

She was waiting in the long, darkly-lit, luxuriously appointed bar when Alastair came to find her; and they sat together, not speaking of the subject on their minds until the waiter had taken their order and had brought them their drinks.

'Now tell me, Cristina,' Alastair said, 'what brought on this sudden disturbance. Sylvana won't say a word.'

'And I *can't*. I honestly have no idea. We had quite a gay morning, a good lunch, and were having coffee on the Champs Elysées, when she got up almost as soon as she had sat down, and said she must leave. She looked ill—pale as a ghost and terribly drawn.'

'Nothing to account for it?'

'Not as far as I know.'

'You hadn't been saying anything to cause her worry or concern?'

'Of course not. You should know better than that.'

'Did she *see* anything to upset her, or anybody she knew?'

'Not as far as I know,' Cristina said again.

Alastair shook his head.

'It isn't the first time,' he said. 'You see, Cristina, the sort of temperament I have to deal with.'

'It's so strange. Couldn't she have some treatment, Alastair?'

'For what? Migraine? Or imaginary troubles she won't speak of?'

'Perhaps they're not imaginary.'

'What else could they be? She's cared for and protected. She certainly has no money troubles. Angus left her quite well-to-do, and I of course intend to provide for her.'

'Even so, with all those advantages, she might be unhappy.'

'Still mourning Angus, do you mean?'

'No, I didn't mean anything specific, but I suppose it could be that.'

'I don't think so. Cristina, I'm going to take you into my confidence. I want to tell you about Sylvana and myself. I think you should understand the position more fully.'

'You said once, Alastair, before we were interrupted, that Sylvana proposed to you, and not the other way round.'

'Yes, but it goes back farther than that. It goes

back to when Angus brought her to meet us up in
Sutherland. My mother lives there, as you know;
and I was spending a longish holiday there. Sylvana was young and very beautiful and very gay;
and it seemed that she and Angus were very much
in love. Angus certainly was. But one day, Sylvana
came to me and said she was making a terrible
mistake: that she loved me and not Angus, and
what should she do about it? It was, to say the
least, a difficult position to be in.'

'Oh yes, how awful!'

'I didn't love her, Cristina. I was fond of her,
but I'd done absolutely nothing to encourage her.
She wept a good deal. I think she felt that if she
loved somebody, that somebody simply must love
her in return. I hated to be stern with her, but I
had to be. It was not only that I didn't love her,
but that Angus did, and she was Angus's girl, and
I had no intention of taking her from him. So
I left Sutherland and went back to my London
house; and in due course they were married and
went to live in Switzerland. Sylvana never liked
Scotland, she thought it grim and cold and inhospit-
able. Angus had inherited an enormous old house
from an uncle, but he never cared for that, so he
sold it and they were able to live in Switzerland in
considerable style; and we saw very little of them
after that. As the children arrived, they sometimes
brought them over to see their grandmother, or my
mother would visit them. I usually contrived to be
somewhere else when they came, but Angus and I
met from time to time; and from what I could
gather, they seemed to have a good and happy
marriage.'

'Although she loved you?' queried Cristina
softly.

'I hoped that was a temporary thing: that she would forget me when I was no longer around. Certainly, Angus didn't seem to miss anything. It was a tragedy when he died from a throat infection against which he stood no chance from the beginning.'

'And Sylvana came straight back to you?'

'Not straight back, no. I was spending a good deal of my time in New York about then. She tried to make her way alone: at first, in Switzerland, then staying with a woman friend in London. This woman, Eva, was divorced and had two children. Sylvana was widowed, with two little boys and a child on the way. They shared a house and seemed to get on well. Well, when I did get back, I went up to Sutherland to see my mother and I found Sylvana and her children there, and she was in very much the same state as she is in to-day.'

'Did you find out why?'

'No. I think, Cristina, that she simply cannot manage life alone.'

'But she isn't managing alone now, Alastair. She has you. It's her own fault that she isn't already married to you. So why is she worrying now?'

'I wish I knew, Cristina, it would make life a lot simpler.'

'And it was then, when you met again in Sutherland, that *she* did the proposing? She must have loved you all the time.'

'I can't say that she exactly proposed. What she did ask me to do was to look after her, to take care of her, not to leave her again. It amounted to the same thing, I suppose. I felt I had a duty to look after her. I hadn't married—I hadn't met a woman I wanted to marry—so I decided to marry Sylvana and look after her and her children.'

'But you still aren't married.'

'No, and God knows why not. I believe honestly, Cristina, that she doesn't really love me, or surely she would have arranged our wedding long before this.'

'Poor Sylvana,' said Cristina thoughtfully. 'And you, Alastair. It seems to me you're sacrificing all you want most from life, in taking on this responsibility of caring for Sylvana. You long to be in Sutherland, and she won't go there. She drags you away from your London house—on a mere whim. She insists you leave Paris—is that also on a mere whim? Why, she would have had you leave there and then, at that moment. Can you live the rest of your life on somebody's whim?'

'She is obviously under strain, she obviously needs care. There doesn't seem to be anybody else to provide it. Now that I know you, Cristina, I wish to God there were. I wish I could hand over this responsibility—although I would always look after them in any other way. I wish I could come to you, free, without obligations, knowing that now I *have* met the woman I want to marry.'

'You've forgotten Vernon again,' she said, and there was a dark unhappiness in her eyes, for Vernon, for herself and for Alastair.

'Yes,' he said. 'I wish that for some short time —a week, a day or an hour—we could forget everybody else, Cristina, and think only of ourselves. God, if I could have you for myself for one short hour!'

They were sitting close together, the arms of their chairs almost touching, but they did not touch. They looked into each other's eyes, looking at the happiness they knew they could share together, and turning away from it.

'You have a heavier burden than I have, Alastair.'

'No, it's an equal burden, to love and have to turn away from it. As far as the children and Sylvana are concerned, I refuse to look upon them as a burden. My life would be unbearable otherwise. I look upon the boys almost as my own, and know that I could take the place of a father for them. Once I can get Sylvana straightened out . . .'

There was a pause. Cristina wondered if he would ever get Sylvana straightened out. She said at last:

'When you go back to the Chateau de la Falaise to-morrow, Alastair, I shall fly to London.'

'No,' he protested quickly; then more slowly: 'Won't you come back with us, Cristina? You could help Sylvana, but it's mostly for my selfish sake that I want you to come. Don't go away from me yet.'

'I don't want to, but I think I must.'

They went into the restaurant for dinner and Alastair said they would discuss no more problems that evening. He talked to her about his Sutherland home. He owned thousands of acres, he told her, most of them unproductive, although more and more were being put down to forestry. He talked to her of fishing days, alone on the lakes in his boat; of stalking days, high in the mountains; of the stone house that held his heart captive. 'It looks forbidding from the outside, but inside we've done everything possible to make it comfortable.' There was more social life than one would expect, considering the remoteness; and he had long since laid down a private airstrip and held a pilot's licence. 'Sylvana won't fly with me. Would *you* come up with me, Cristina?' he asked her; and when she replied promptly: 'Of course I would,' he smiled at her with a swift, intimate charm that seemed to turn her heart over.

'Dreams, dreams, dreams,' she said, and there was an unaccustomed wistfulness in her voice.

Only one thing broke into their solitude that was yet not a solitude because they were surrounded by other people; and that was when he left her for a few moments to go and see how Sylvana was, and returned to report her sleeping. And at long last they went up in the lift together and Alastair escorted her to her room, opened the door and went in with her and closed the door again behind him.

The maid had left one bedside light switched on, but it was dim and golden in the room. Inside the door, Alastair took Cristina into his arms and she put hers round his neck and leaned against him, saying softly: 'Darling, darling . . .' They kissed again and again.

'How can I leave you?' he whispered urgently into her hair.

'You must,' she said. 'Alastair, it would always be like this. We have to put an end to it. I shall go to London in the morning.'

She thought her mind was irrevocably made up, when at last he left her alone in her room; and yet, in the morning, she was weak against Sylvana's continued pleading to her to return to the chateau with them. In the end she went back instead of going to London. Just for a day or two, she told herself, to see if she really could be of help to Sylvana.

As they drove away from Paris, Sylvana's anxiety and fear seemed to lessen. The farther they went into the rural countryside, the better she seemed to feel. By the time she reached the chateau, all the lines of strain had disappeared from her face, leaving it the customary smooth and beautiful oval. She greeted the children as if she had not seen them for a month, picking up Jennifer and holding her in her arms, refusing to part with her even when Alastair said: 'She's heavy for you, Sylvana, let her walk.' Cristina felt she had been induced to return with them under false pretences. She was not needed now. Was it simply separation from her children that had upset Sylvana? It hardly seemed likely, but certainly being reunited with them had a wonderfully recuperative effect.

That evening, from the solitude of her own house, she telephoned Vernon.

'Well, how is Paris?' he asked her after the usual greetings. 'Are you having an extravagant whirl?'

'No, the Paris prices horrify me. I helped Sylvana to have one. But the fact is, Vernon, that we're not in Paris now. We're back at the chateau.'

'But why?' he demanded. 'Why aren't you coming home? Don't you know you're needed here?'

'Yes, yes, I do know, and I was all set to come. But Sylvana was seized with some strange sort of upset—I honestly don't know what to call it except a *crise de nerfs*—ill with migraine and anxiety and some sort of stress; and simply pleaded with me to come back with her. And then, the moment she was back here, she recovered miraculously, and I feel very hard done by!'

'That family imposes upon you, Cristie.'

'I know. I seem to have let myself get involved.'

'Then please get uninvolved, and come home. *I* need you more than they do.'

'I haven't got a home, let me remind you.'

'Wherever I am, you have a home. Our house

157

in the country, my flat in town. "Come live with me and be my love, and we will all the pleasures prove".'

'Who could refuse such a charming invitation? Yes, I will come. I'll wait a couple of days, to straighten up here and see that Sylvana is really better, and then I'll drive back.'

Yes, she thought, as she put the receiver back on its cradle, she had let herself get involved all too deeply with the Buchanan family, and the sooner she returned to Vernon the better it would be for all concerned.

Hard on the heels of this sensible thought came the ringing of her doorbell, and there on the doorstep was Alastair.

'Sylvana insists on your coming to dinner,' he said. 'Neither of us can bear the thought of you eating here alone, especially as we were the cause of bringing you back.'

'I don't like the thought much myself,' she said. 'Especially as there's nothing to have for dinner, unless I open a tin. Thank you, I shall be pleased to come.'

He had stepped into the hallway. Now he closed the door behind him.

'You've seen yourself, Cristina, that Sylvana now seems to be quite well. I do apologise for upsetting your arrangements. You have too kind a heart. You must find us a great nuisance.'

'No, not a nuisance. A great disturbance, yes. I've just been speaking to Vernon on the phone, and I've promised him that I will go home.'

'Yes, I'm sure that's the best thing.' They looked at each other knowing that it was not the best thing, but the only possible one.

'Please go,' Cristina said quickly. 'I'll follow

you.'

' You don't trust me,' he said quietly.

' I don't trust myself.' The longing for him was so much that suddenly she said intensely: ' Don't you *see* that all I want is for us to be together? Nobody else. Just you and I. You and I. Oh, Alastair!'

Without any conscious movement, they were in each other's arms again.

' I can understand Sylvana wanting you,' she went on rapidly, ' for I want you myself. I can understand her falling out of love with Angus and in love with you, because *I* thought I loved Vernon, but I've fallen in love with you. I went to Paris simply to see you a little longer. Darling, can't you come back here later to-night—to be with me?'

There was a long silence. Then Alastair released her, and stood looking down at her very seriously.

' Yes, I could come back here,' he said quietly, ' if I wanted to upset the whole applecart. Do you think I don't *want* to come? And would you like to go back to Vernon with that on your conscience? Wouldn't it make it harder to go back at all? And how soon would you begin to regret it, and begin to hate me for it? . . . Come along.' Suddenly his voice was harsh. ' Let's go over to dinner. And I won't come to-night. We'll both lie awake instead wishing for something we can't have.' He opened the door and would not listen to her protestations that she wasn't ready, but went with her across to his own house. Quite stern now, Cristina thought. Perhaps she had shocked him, or perhaps he was having his own struggle with temptation. Whatever the reason, he was, for the rest of the evening, withdrawn, uncommunicative, unapproachable.

Sylvana, however, was obviously her old self

again. She had kept the boys up to say good-night to Cristina, and they joined in the aperitifs with a natural, attractive charm, drinking their black-currant drink soberly, passing round the small delicacies, trying to extract a promise from Cristina that she would ride with them in the morning.

'I'm going back to England to-morrow,' she told them, smiling.

'But you've only just *come*,' Neil protested.

'I've just come from Paris, but I've been away from England a long time.'

'Ride in the morning and go back to England afterwards,' suggested Angus. 'It's awfully quiet with all your friends gone away.'

She could not bear to disappoint them. She promised to ride in the morning.

The evening was not a success. Alastair was withdrawn. Sylvana was thoughtful, inclined to retreat into silences. Cristina gave up the attempt to make conversation, and decided to leave after they had had their coffee. When she rose to go, Sylvana said good-night and Alastair saw her to the door.

'That was not very polite of you, Alastair,' Sylvana said. 'You should at least have taken her to her own door.'

'She knows the way,' Alastair said shortly.

CHAPTER VIII

Sylvana came out to the stables next morning to see them set off for their morning ride. This was very unusual, for she always gave the horses a wide berth, and even now was careful to keep Jennifer from getting near to any of them. It was difficult this morning, for Firebrand was excessively fiery, prancing about while the ponies were being saddled and doing his best to unseat Alastair.

'He's been missing his exercise,' Alastair said, mastering him with no little difficulty.

'He's showing off,' said six-year-old Neil seriously, as Firebrand reared up, pawing the air with his forelegs.

'He'll settle down in a while. All right, Cristina?'

'Fine. But you go first, please, and keep out of our way until Firebrand quietens down. Angus and Neil, you and I will follow. Goodbye, Sylvana.'

'Goodbye. Have a nice ride. Boys, bring Cristina back to lunch.'

'We will,' they promised, and set off in a small cavalcade across the stable yard; Alastair way ahead, determined to get the better of Firebrand's burning impatience, the others following. The clatter of the hooves on the stone cobble ended at the wide gate, and Sylvana followed with little Jennifer, watching as they all picked their way down the sloping road—not so steep on this side of the plateau—towards the fields. She watched for a long time: Alastair with his proud, confident seat, the two boys always trying to imitate him, Cristina not nearly so confident. She watched until the slow curve of the road took them from her sight, then she slowly turned, holding Jennifer by the hand, and they went back to the house.

Cristina was sorry to leave her behind, for it would surely be better if she could share some of Alastair's interests. Even if she did not like Scotland and his country life there, she could have learned to ride in France, have ridden with her future husband and her sons. She herself was not a good rider, having come to it late; but if *she* were married to Alastair, she would ride every day until she improved enough to be a good companion for him.

That morning they all enjoyed their ride. Alastair in particular had a rousing gallop. Firebrand going furiously as if the devil were at his heels, while the others watched and waited. And when he returned, Alastair was triumphant. 'That's taken some of the fire out of him,' he said, and it was true. Firebrand was much more quiescent. They were all glowing, and all hungry for lunch, when at last they returned to the stables.

'You go back to the house, Cristina,' said Alastair, 'and we'll help Jean-Pierre with the horses.' The boys, who did not particularly like the work of rubbing down, were happy to do it when Alastair was with them. Cristina left them and went to the house to find Sylvana. She was nowhere about, so she went upstairs to a bathroom to wash and see to her make-up and her hair. When she went down again, she found Marthe putting finishing touches to the dining table.

'*Bonjour*, Marthe. Where is Madame Buchanan?'

'She went out, *m'selle*.'

Cristina saw that only four places were laid at
162

the luncheon table.

'She is not coming back to lunch?'

'No, *m'selle.*'

'And Jennifer and Marguerite?'

'They all went. The village taxi came for them. Madame took Jennifer, and Marguerite has the rest of the day off.'

Marthe's French was always difficult to understand, but Cristina understood that amount. She went into the sitting room, wondering why Sylvana had not mentioned that she was going out. Or had she made up her mind impulsively, on finding herself left alone?

Alastair and the boys were also surprised to find her gone.

'I expect she's gone shopping,' said Angus.

'I hardly think she'd need to shop here after being in Paris,' Alastair told him. 'But she didn't need to call on the village taxi. I would have taken her where she wanted to go.'

As the day turned out, it was very doubtful if Alastair would have taken her. For Sylvana did not return during the course of the afternoon, nor had she arrived by Jennifer's usual bedtime. 'She'll be here soon,' said Alastair. 'She never keeps Jennifer up late. I'll ring the taxi-driver and find out if she booked him and for what time.'

He did this, and came back to where Cristina was watching the boys with their car-racing game, and said:

'That's very odd. He took Sylvana down with Jennifer this morning and says she had a great deal of luggage with her. I wonder if Marthe knows anything about this.'

Marthe, however, knew nothing. She knew the taxi-driver had called, because Marguerite was up-

163

stairs with Madame and had not bothered to come down and answer the doorbell. ' But after that,' she said, ' I went back to my kitchen. *I* don't know how much luggage Madame had with her. I was too busy to have time to poke my nose into her affairs.'

' Perhaps Mummy's gone back to Paris,' said Neil.

' That's hardly likely,' said Alastair, remembering how anxious she had been to get away from it.

Further consultation with the old French taxi-driver elicited the information that he had driven Madame and the child and the *mademoiselle* to the nearest large town, where she had asked to be directed to a car-hire firm. He had brought Marguerite back to the village, and that was the end of it, that was all he knew. Yes, she did have a considerable amount of baggage.

' Surely she would have left a note if she meant to stay away,' suggested Cristina.

' She hasn't given one to Marthe.'

' In her room, perhaps? You haven't actually looked for one, have you?'

Alastair went upstairs at once, and returned waving a letter with an air of shamefaced embarrassment. ' Why didn't *I* think of that?' he asked. ' And hours ago?'

' I suppose she hasn't done *this* before,' said Cristina. ' What does she say?'

' So little that I find it infuriating.' He passed the letter to Cristina and it was indeed irritatingly short.

' My dear, dear Alastair,' she wrote,

' My life is in a dreadful muddle. You have always been so, so kind to me, and I would have wanted to stay with you always. But it is im-

164

possible, quite impossible. I am taking my
darling Jennifer and going back to my mama and
papa in Calabria. Papa will always look after
me, and you will no longer have to undertake
this task, which must have been often difficult for
you.

'I did not take the boys away from you,
because I am certain that their happiness and all
their future good lies with you. If I am wrong,
you will of course let me know, and we will
arrange to bring them to Italy. I am sorry for
all the trouble I have given you, and so so grateful to you for all your kindness.

'Your loving Sylvana.'

'What sort of explanation is that?' demanded
Alastair.

'Where's Mummy? What is the matter with
her?' asked Neil anxiously.

'There's nothing the matter with her,' Alastair
reassured him. 'She's gone to stay with your grandmother and grandfather in Calabria for a while.'

'When is she coming back?'

'She doesn't say. I think she would like to stay
there for a while. Do you want to go there, too?'

'I don't,' put in Angus. 'I want to stay with
you.'

'What about you, Neil? Your mother says that
if you like to go, she will arrange it.'

Neil looked slightly harassed.

'I want to stay with Angus,' he said at last.

'Perhaps we could go and see her for a little
while,' he added undecidedly.

'Of course, whenever you want to,' said Alastair
cheerfully.

'Oh. Then I think I'll stay here,' said Neil.
'But who will look after us?'

'Marguerite will be back in the morning. She'll come up with the croissants and the bread.'

Neil apparently found this mundane statement quite reassuring, and went off with Angus to the kitchen so that Marthe could give them their supper. Both Alastair and Cristina went upstairs with them later, to see them through their baths and into their beds; and it was not until they went down again and Alastair had poured a drink for each of them, that they discussed Sylvana's letter together.

'What does she mean,' asked Cristina, 'by writing that her life is in a dreadful muddle?'

'This is what I intend to find out. I shall have to go after her, of course.'

'I suppose so. You don't think, Alastair, that she found out about the way *we* feel?'

'The way we feel about each other? I very much doubt it. Sylvana is very self-absorbed. No, it must be something else altogether.' He reflected for some time on Sylvana's conduct, and on past incidents, while Cristina watched him and waited. At last, he said:

'Looking back, I realise that she has always acted as if she had to escape from something. She wanted to escape from London, she wanted to escape from society, and retreat into the quietest place we could find; she wanted to escape from Paris. And now she is escaping again. Her father will spoil her, of course. He would have liked to keep her for ever; and will be glad she has gone home. He'll treat her like a child, and only having Jennifer to look after will keep her from becoming one. . . . Well, I'd better go after her as soon as possible. The problem is: what shall I do with the boys in the meantime?'

'They can't stay here with Marguerite?'

'They could, but I sense an insecurity in them already, especially in Neil. No, I don't think that will do. Either I send them back to Sutherland, to my mother, or take them with me to Italy, to their own. Would *you* take them to Sutherland for me, Cristina?'

'Yes.' She sighed a sharp sigh. 'I promised Vernon I would uninvolve myself.'

'Yes, yes, of course. I'm asking too much of you. You go home to Vernon, who has been very patient.'

'I don't think I can do that,' Cristina told him. 'I can't, somehow, *get* myself uninvolved. I don't want Neil to feel insecure. I want to know what happens to you all. I want to know why Sylvana's life is such a muddle.'

He held out his arms to her, and she walked into their embrace.

'Come with us, then, darling Cristina. We'll all go to Italy, you and I and Angus and Neil. If you have to go back immediately afterwards, at least we shall have had this journey together.'

'I shall have to talk it over with Vernon first,' she said.

'I know what *he* will say. I know what any man worth his salt would say.'

'He's very understanding.'

'But there's a limit to understanding.'

'We'll see,' she said.

There was a delay in getting a line to England, but at last, in the seclusion of her oval room in her own house, Cristina heard Vernon's voice.

'Hello there, Cristie! Nice to hear your voice again. You must be spending a fortune on phone calls.'

'Well, this one is fairly urgent.'

167

'Don't say you're not coming home yet,' he warned her.

'But that *is* just what I'm going to say . . .'

'No, don't,' he said sharply.

'Oh, Vernon, it's just that strange things have been happening here . . .'

'Very strange, to my way of thinking, if they keep you away so long.'

'Listen, darling. I'm sure you'll be sympathetic when you know. Sylvana has run away to Italy, and Alastair feels he has to go after her . . .'

Once more he interrupted.

'That's his pigeon, it has nothing to do with you.'

'In a way, it is; because it's made the little boys feel very insecure, and . . .'

'Alastair can look after them. He's not incapable. Cristie, Cristie, you're still being involved. Cut loose and come home and let them look after themselves.'

'I can't do that, Vernon. I feel an obligation to them.'

'That's nonsense. You're under no obligation.'

'But what difference does it make, Vernon, whether I come this week or next?'

'You can ask that, Cristie? You can ask *me* that?'

'Well, we have got the rest of our life in front of us. And I can be of use here.'

'What use can you be?'

'Chiefly in reassuring the boys. I was going with them to Italy.'

'What!'

She repeated her words.

'Who's them?' asked Vernon. 'The boys, or the boys and Buchanan?'

'All of them,' said Cristina, and knew that she
168

had made a mistake.

'Cristina,' said Vernon; and by his calling her by her full name and calling Alastair Buchanan, she knew that this was serious. 'Come home to-morrow.'

There was a long pause. 'Are you there?' asked Vernon.

'Yes, I'm here,' she said, and her throat was suddenly dry.

'You come home to-morrow, or you needn't come at all.'

'Darling,' she cried, 'you don't understand.'

'I understand very well that something is going on there that I don't like. I don't see any need for you to be involved at all. Cristina, you come home to-morrow or you needn't come at all.'

'I see,' she said quietly. 'I see.'

'And which is it going to be?' he asked her.

'I'll come home,' she said, feeling unutterably sad.

'Well, don't sound like a damned martyr about it,' he shouted. She knew that he was very angry, and he had a right to be. 'I don't want any martyrs round me. I don't want to be a penance for anybody. Just make up your mind, Cristina.' And he rang off, leaving her in a sea of desolation.

So she tossed and turned restlessly for most of the night.

Early in the morning she got up and packed. When the baker's van arrived, bringing a fresh-cheeked, bright-eyed Marguerite as well as the croissants and rolls, she made herself eat a breakfast of coffee and croissants, and then carried her bags into the hall. She switched off the boiler and the fridge, and went round the house making sure that all the doors and windows were locked or closed.

As she was carrying the first of her bags out to the car, Angus and Neil arrived to see her.

'Where are you going, Cristina?' cried Angus.

'I have to go back to England,' she said.

'Oh, please, *please* come to Italy with us,' persuaded Neil.

'But you have your uncle to take you, and you're going to see your mother and Jennifer.'

'But we want *you* to come,' they assured her. 'We came to find out when you would be ready to start.'

She shook her head.

'You're going to see your mother and your grandparents. There's no need for me to be there. But I'm sure I'll see you some time soon.'

They went away dejected, aware of the fact that something strange was going on in their world, but not knowing what it was. Everybody seemed to be going away, there was too much coming and going for them to feel happy about it.

Cristina was not surprised when Alastair came soon after the boys.

'So you're going?' he asked quietly.

'Yes.'

'Vernon didn't approve of the Italian trip?'

'No, very much the reverse.'

'I would be the same in his position. One wouldn't expect him to like it. So this is goodbye, Cristina, is it?'

'It seems so. I can't bear to let you all go without me.'

'But you can't be in two places at once, and you can't be all things to all men. What did Vernon say?'

'He said that if I didn't go home to-day I needn't go at all.'

'Then of course you must go. Oh, Cristina, if I were a free man, I wouldn't be standing on the sidelines like this, powerless to intervene. You may be sure of that. But how can I let Sylvana down, or the boys? The boys may well be my responsibility for the rest of my life. It's Jennifer who absorbs nearly all Sylvana's devotion, and I think the boys, young as they are, have always sensed it.'

'I know. I know what your obligations are, Alastair, and I know you'd never shirk them.'

'But what if Sylvana's letter has a grain of sense in it, Cristina? What if there *is* something that makes it impossible for her to stay with me? Then I might be a free man after all. What then, Cristina, what then?'

'My promises to Vernon,' she said.

'Then it *is* goodbye?'

'Yes,' she said; and stretched her hands out before her to keep him at arm's length. He took a deep breath, looked at her for a long time, then slowly turned and went away, out of the door, across the lawns. Out of her life, thought Cristina. Was it possible to let him walk away from her like that, everything over between them?

Vernon could not mean what he said, she thought. He could not mean it. Even if she went to Italy with Alastair and the boys, he would come to understand it, even if he did not now. Should she allow him to dictate her actions, set a precedent he might expect her to follow all through their married life? Surely she had a right to do this one thing she wanted to do. She was dragged so much in two directions that she felt she was no longer seeing things clearly. She got into her car and drove to the heavy gates.

It was nearly an hour later that the gleaming

white Rolls-Royce arrived at the gates, and Angus jumped out to open them. Alastair also got out of the driving seat, walking to the French car in front of him. 'We'll open the gate for you,' he said, looking at Cristina curiously.

'I can't let you go without me,' she said. 'I've been waiting here an hour, with my courage draining away. A few more minutes and I would have gone.'

Angus was struggling with the big gates. He turned as Alastair called to him.

'Come along, Angus, help us with the luggage. Cristina is coming with us.'

He whooped with delight. The atmosphere suddenly lightened. They all became unnecessarily busy, transferring all Cristina's possessions to the boot of the big car. 'Will we have enough food in the picnic hamper?' asked Neil anxiously.

'Oh, I don't eat *that* much,' Cristina assured him, smiling at him. She went to help Angus push open the tall and heavy gates, the big car drove through. Alastair took Cristina's car back to his own garage and returned to the Rolls.

Cristina sat in front with Alastair, the two boys at the back, and the car glided along the French roads almost as on a cushion of air.

'What luxury,' Cristina said.

'We look like a nice family,' Angus pronounced.

'Well, there's a smug young man for you,' Alastair commented.

'What does smug mean?' Neil wanted to know.

Cristina threw her doubts overboard. The die was cast now. She was on her way, and it was no use mulling over possible consequences. She was sure that Vernon hadn't meant his ultimatum. When she returned to England, he would understand and forgive her. She simply had to know what was happening, what was going to happen, in this Buchanan family.

They had their picnic lunch. They crossed into Italy later in the day, by which time Angus was in front with Alastair, and Neil was leaning against Cristina in the back, tired but apparently content. She had an arm about him. She thought Angus was the confident one, Neil more anxious. It was Neil who needed comfort and reassurance.

Both boys were asleep by the time they stopped for the night. At the hotel, Italian porters ran round obligingly at sight of the Rolls, and willingly carried the boys up to their room. They woke, but were reassured by the sight of Alastair and went to bed together in a big double bed, satisfied. Alastair and Cristina waited until they were asleep again and went down to dinner.

' The hotel staff were quite disturbed to discover that you were not Signora Buchanan,' Alastair told Cristina.

' They probably think I'm the governess or the nanny,' she said.

' Or my mistress,' said Alastair, but Cristina chose not to follow up this provocative suggestion. Nor would she walk in the hotel garden after dinner, to get a little fresh air, for she knew what that would lead to, and she was trying to retain a modicum of common sense. She was tired, she said, after such a long and decision-making day, and would go early to bed.

Next morning they were up and away very early and sweeping with swift ease along the autostrada from north to south, 'gobbling up' Italy, Angus said, to get to his mother. But it was late in the day when they reached the village in Calabria where Sylvana's parents lived, and drove through it to the outskirts where a handsome and roomy Italian villa stood in its pleasant garden.

From this moment on Cristina felt curiously out of everything. The welcome was vociferous, as only an Italian welcome could be. Such kissings and exclamations! The boys were hugged over and over again. The Italian language, which Cristina did not understand, flowed over her in a melodious river of sound. Jennifer was in bed, but everybody else seemed to be talking at once: question and answer and explanation, and considerable surprise that Cristina should be there at all. Sylvana had gone very pale, but did not seem as surprised to see Alastair as Cristina would have expected. Had she expected him to follow? Was this also a pattern of behaviour on her part?

It was discovered that they had not had dinner, and a plump, middle-aged woman, presumably the cook, was called in, and once more the boys were hugged and kissed, and a loquacious conversation about the supper was carried on. As they later sat at their meal with the boys, Cristina said to Alastair: 'Of course I haven't understood a thing. You'll have to translate for me.'

'So far, nothing of importance. Sylvana's parents apparently think of this as an ordinary visit. I'll have a showdown with Sylvana in the morning.'

The 'showdown' when it arrived included Cristina also, at Sylvana's request; and since there seemed little likelihood of privacy in such an exuberant household, it took place at an hotel at some distance from her home to which they drove in the Rolls, and where they stopped for coffee. They were the only occupants of a pleasant, vine-covered terrace.

Sylvana said:

'I had little sleep last night, Alastair. I was thinking very seriously, and I know now that the only thing for me to do is to tell you the truth.'

'That surely doesn't mean you have been lying to me?'

'No, I have never lied, but I kept the truth from you. And my only reason for doing that is that I never wanted to do without your protection.'

'I can't think of anything that would make me withdraw my protection. Suppose you start then, Sylvana, by telling us this truth that you have so far withheld.'

She hesitated. Then she looked at Cristina with a doubtful smile, then back at Alastair.

'I still find it so hard,' she said, and took a deep breath. 'Alastair, the reason why I would never fix a date for our wedding was that I am already married.'

He looked sharply at her.

'You're not referring to Angus?' he asked, making sure.

'No, I'm not referring to Angus. I am referring to the man I married after Angus died; the man I ran away from when I came to you in Sutherland; the man who still terrifies me. I knew he was in London, which was why I wanted to get away from there. I saw him last week in Paris. I am sure he is looking for me still.'

This was indeed a bombshell. They looked at her in disbelief, wondering if they were to take her words seriously.

'But this is incredible, Sylvana. Tell me how it happened.'

'Alastair, you can't imagine how *alone* I felt when Angus died. I know you were kind, and so

175

was your mother; but I went on living in our house in Switzerland with the two little boys, knowing I was going to have another baby, feeling so deserted and unable to manage; and this man, Charles Hardwicke, who had known us when Angus was alive, seemed to be such a tower of strength. He was always coming to see me, to see if I was all right; always taking the boys out for treats, often coming late in the evening, when I used to feel particularly lonely, to cheer me up. I began to rely on him. He was very forceful. It might be difficult for you to understand how he swept me into things, but he had a very powerful personality. He asked me to marry him, but I thought it was much too soon after Angus's death, and said No. And when Eva invited me to share her house in London, because she was just divorced and was feeling rather bad about it, and she had her children to look after too, I thought it was a very good idea, and so I went to London. I left the Swiss house for an agent to sell, as you know.'

She paused momentarily, and Cristina thought that this unaccustomed rush of words would afford Sylvana immense relief.

'But Charles Hardwicke followed me there,' Sylvana went on. 'He gave me little peace, and he seemed to be so devoted, and said I needed somebody to care for me and he would be happy to do so. Well, in the end I said Yes, and we were married.

'But then! Then he changed completely. Once we were married, he didn't even pretend to love me. All he wanted was to get his hands on my money, and he was so clever that he thought of all sorts of ways to do it. He knew all about your family and your estates, and all about Angus's affairs—I don't know how. And he stole my jewellery and sold that; and he laughed at me for being so stupid as not to see through him. And what I could *not* forgive was that he was unkind to the boys. They were a nuisance to him. And soon I was a nuisance too. But when he started to—to ill-treat me, I had had enough. Eva kept saying: " leave him, leave him ". I thought of going home to Mama and Papa, but I didn't want to bring them trouble; and Eva said: " Go to Alastair. He will look after you. He will settle this Hardwicke's hash." And so I waited until Charles was away, and I packed up all my things, and all the children's, and I came to you.'

' Then why didn't you tell me the truth then, Sylvana?'

' I thought you might think I should go back to my husband. Or that you might want to tackle him, and make trouble. And to tell you the truth, Alastair, I was ashamed of myself for marrying so soon after Angus died. All these things. And also, of course, that when I saw you again, I loved you so much that I didn't *want* to tell you; to appear so spoiled in your eyes, so tarnished.'

' You should have known that you could rely on my sympathy and help, my dear.'

' I know, but I never seem to do the right thing. I always seem to act so stupidly. I can't *manage* my life, Alastair; and I thought you would manage it for me. . . . But now I know how stupid I was. I couldn't marry you myself, but I was preventing you marrying anybody else. It was crazy. But now I think Papa will look after me. I shall live here with Jennifer and make my life with my parents.'

' You can be divorced from this man, Sylvana.'

' No. I am Catholic. So is he, and would not hear of it. No, Alastair, I will never marry again.'

There was a long silence. Sylvana was conscious of her relief that at last the truth was out, relief too that she was home again with her parents. She had never really grown to maturity, and her parents might have been partly the cause of that: they would continue to care for her as their child.

Cristina had a certain sympathy for Sylvana, who, for all her beauty, was one of those people constantly buffeted by fate; but she had more anger. Anger because Alastair had given up so much of his life and care to her; given up his London house to stay cut off at the Chateau de la Falaise; given up the place he loved most in the world, his house in Sutherland. And on top of these feelings, the reluctant sympathy and the anger, she admitted the realisation that Alastair was, after all, free.

What Alastair himself was feeling she could not tell. Was he also looking at the wasted months? Was he even now looking at this unexpected freedom and what it might entail? Cristina would not look at him. She looked at Sylvana, who now appeared calm and purged, beautiful and childlike. She heard Alastair say:

'Angus and Neil, Sylvana. Why did you leave them with me?'

'Don't you want to have them, Alastair?'

'Don't *you*?'

'Oh yes, but they are not little Italian boys, Alastair. They are Scots, like you. They don't like Italy. They don't like to be hugged and kissed by Mama and Papa. They like to be in the mountains with you, fishing and climbing and riding horses. They would be so much happier with you.'

'All boys need a mother's care, Sylvana.'

'They can come and see me sometimes. You would allow that?'

'That's hardly the same thing.'

'But you said yourself we have to consider their schooling. They will soon be at school; perhaps, in your heartless English way, away at a boarding school. And also, Alastair, you might get married and then they would have another mother.'

'What a simple view of life you have, Sylvana. Not all women want to mother somebody else's children.'

'But Cristina would. She loves the boys.'

This was indeed a bombshell; quite as much as the news of Sylvana's married state. Cristina said:

'You've forgotten, Sylvana, that *I* am going to marry Vernon.'

'Then you would be crazy and stupid, too. You should marry Alastair.'

Alastair rose to his feet.

'Come along, both of you. We're going to see if this hotel can give us lunch. And Sylvana has not made such a great success of running her own life that she can now start to run Cristina's.'

'I know I'm not very clever,' Sylvana said, rising to go into the hotel with them, 'but I do know that you should never let real love pass you by; because it doesn't happen all that often.'

Alastair and Cristina suddenly found themselves looking into each other's eyes.

'I apologise to Sylvana,' said Alastair. 'She's right. It doesn't happen all that often.'

'And perhaps one should never let it pass one by,' added Cristina.

As they sat at lunch, Cristina's thoughts would have concentrated on how these revelations would have affected her own life, but that Alastair had not yet finished with the subject of the husband whose

179

existence had so recently been made known to them.

'Sylvana, you say you wanted to leave London because this Hardwicke was living there; you brought us back from Paris in a hurry because you saw him there. But you have no evidence that he was looking for you, that he was still interested in you.'

'Only that I know him. I know he is mean and cruel and greedy. You know, when I came to Scotland, I couldn't find my cheque book, so I applied to the bank for a new one. But Charles had it and he forged all the cheques in it, for quite a lot of money, Alastair. You know I never keep any sort of accounts, I am very stupid about figures. I never knew what was happening until the bank manager wrote to say I would have to transfer some things. . . . And once Charles said he would take the boys away from me. I don't think he meant it, but I couldn't be sure. And I was always afraid that he would take the boys away, or darling Jennifer, and ask for a ransom or something like that. That was why I had to come back from Paris, to make sure they were safe.'

'Poor Sylvana!' said Cristina.

Alastair sighed and spread out his hands with a kind of despair.

'Why you couldn't have trusted me with the truth, I shall never know: why you endured these fears and anxieties alone, probably unnecessarily, when I could have set your mind at rest. You can leave Hardwicke to me. If there's any risk at all of his pestering you, the law can stop him if I can't. If he did forge the cheques, he can be prosecuted for that. Don't worry any more, Sylvana. There are ways of coping with rats like him.'

When they returned to the villa of Sylvana's

parents, Sylvana seemed much more composed. Cristina believed she might be placidly happy in the company of her family and Jennifer; and indeed hoped so, since the marriage to Alastair was now known by all three of them to be impossible. Only somebody as naïve as Sylvana would have kept the engagement going so long, knowing there could be no end result. But if Sylvana's immediate future was taken care of, what about her own? She had now to look at her own problems.

CHAPTER IX

Alastair and Cristina were back at the Chateau de
la Falaise, and the young boys were with them, so
there had been little chance of private and serious
conversation. Nor, although the attraction between them was as powerful as ever, had they
allowed themselves to give it the slightest rein.
The fact that Alastair was a free man made all the
difference. While he was bound, he could feel, and
say to Cristina: ' Just this once, Cristina, just this
once,' when he took her into his arms. Now he
knew that he had no right to influence her life or
her decisions; for she was still bound.

Angus and Neil had been invited to stay with
their grandparents in Calabria for a long holiday
and they were curiously uneasy about it, sensing
that something was not as usual. Couldn't Alastair
stay too? No, he was busy, he had his work to do.
Couldn't he do it here in Italy as well as in France?
No, it wasn't possible. Then couldn't Mummy
come back, too? No again. Their mother wanted
to be in Italy.

Angus had decided. He would go back with
Alastair to the chateau, to Scotland with him
later, then to school. Neil had decided with great
reluctance, wanting to be with his mother, wanting
to be with Angus. In the end, he went too. He sat
with Cristina in the back of the car, Cristina keeping him occupied, talking to him, not daring
overtly to console him, but assuring him that he
could always go to Italy for long holidays.

At the chateau, they separated for their different
houses. The boys had Marguerite, always spark-

ling and merry, to receive them; Marthe to make the house seem normal. Cristina found her house quiet, unlived-in, lonely. And she knew that she must get in touch with Vernon as soon as possible. That first evening, tired from the long drive, vaguely depressed, she did not want to do it; and when she finally tried to call him, all the lines were engaged, and she had to sit and wait in the quiet room of the tower for more than two hours. In that time, she speculated on how he would now be feeling. Surely he would no longer be angry about the trip to Italy. She had known Vernon angry about various things—but never with her—but his anger always passed quickly. He had a kind, ungrudging, tolerant personality.

When the bell finally rang, it startled her. She jumped from her seat to answer it.

'Oh, Vernon, is that you?' she cried across the miles.

'It is,' he answered.

'This is Cristina.'

'I haven't quite forgotten your voice,' he said drily.

This was not exactly an auspicious beginning. She hesitated.

'Where are you now, Cristina? Paris, the chateau, Italy, or have you found it necessary to run off to Morocco or Timbuctoo?'

'Oh, Vernon! I'm at the chateau.'

'At your house? Or his?'

'At my house. Alone.'

'But you went to Italy?'

'Yes.'

'Although you promised me you would come home?'

'Vernon darling, there were good reasons.' But

183

she could not think at that moment what her good reasons had been. 'And Vernon, the most extraordinary thing! Sylvana was married all the time, to some dreadful man who pressganged her after her husband died. And *that* was why she would never set a date for marrying Alastair. She just couldn't marry him. And that was why she was always so nervous . . .'

'Cristina!' He was shouting at her. 'Will you stop talking about these people! Don't you realise I'm not in the least interested in anything about them? Let them sort out their muddles themselves. What *I'm* interested in is the fact that they come first with you. If *I* came first, you would have come home when I asked you to. If *I* came first, you would be here with me, sorting out *our* future lives, not the life of a beautiful-but-dumb creature who's practically a stranger to you.'

'Vernon, it isn't like that at all . . .'

'Of course it's like that. And how do I know that it wouldn't be just the same at any other time? It was a bad day for me, Cristina, when you inherited your grandmother's fortune. It gave you independence to do what you like, whether I like it or not. And now you tell me this Buchanan is free. What difference does that make to *us*, Cristina?'

'Oh, Vernon, none at all.'

'Ha,' he said. 'You love the man.'

It was not a question but a statement. There was no reply she could think of to it, nothing she could say.

'Does he love you?' Vernon wanted to know.

'Vernon, let me come home and talk to you.'

'Does he, does he? Answer my question.'

'I believe so.'

'You believe so. And you say it makes no
184

difference to us! When you didn't come home, Cristina, I knew what it meant. You wouldn't have gone tearing off to Italy if you'd loved me. I said it then, and I say it again now. Don't bother to come home on my account.'

'Vernon, you can't mean it.'

'I can and I do. I'm not playing second fiddle for anybody. At least nobody will be able to say I married you for your money—after all. And I suppose they can't say it about him since he seems to be rolling in it. Well, goodbye, Cristina, I think we've said it all.'

'I haven't had an opportunity to say anything yet,' she cried.

'What *can* you say? Honestly, Cristie, what can you say, except: Thanks, Vernon, it's been lovely, but it's over because I've met somebody else. Come on, what can you say, except goodbye?'

She recognised the pain behind his accusing voice, and she could not find an answer. He said slowly:

'All right then, Cristie. Goodbye.' And rang off.

He had called her Cristie again at the end. He was more hurt than he would admit, but he had saved his pride. She sat in her beautiful, lonely, round tower room, and wept.

Early next morning Angus and Neil came to her house early, even before the arrival of the van with the loaves and croissants, to invite her to breakfast. She was glad to go with them, glad to sit with them at the table waiting for Alastair to arrive. He looked at her quickly, saw the dark shadows under her eyes, guessed at the sleepless night, and said sympathetically: 'Was it rough, Cristina?'

185

'Very rough.'

'Are you leaving?'

The boys looked up quickly, awaiting her answer. She shook her head.

'Were you going somewhere?' asked Neil.

'I thought I might be going to London.'

'And now you're not?'

'Now I'm not,' she said, and only Alastair recognised the grief behind that simple statement.

'Well, that's fine,' said Alastair, deliberately assuming a pleased and spirited air, 'because you'll be able to come with us when we go, won't she, boys?'

'Where are *we* going?' they asked, wide-eyed, not knowing yet whether they were going to be pleased or anxious again.

'I think it's time we went to Sutherland again, don't you? Soon it will be time for the grouse! And we haven't been out on the lakes for quite a long time. It's time we took Cristina up there to show her our mountains and our beaches, and to introduce her to your Scottish grandmother, and to show her our house. What do you think?'

'Yes, yes!' they cried, immediately enthusiastic. The house in Sutherland was a sheet-anchor, something they loved and recognised as safe. They plunged immediately into plans with Alastair, and Cristina sat back and listened to them, not daring as yet to look at a new happiness, still looking backward sorrowfully at an old one. But she heard Alastair say:

'I don't think we shall need a house in France at all. Perhaps we will give it back to Cristina.'

She roused herself to say:

'I think perhaps I won't need a house in France either.'

186

' Then let's sell them both to somebody else,' said Neil practically.

After breakfast, Marguerite came to take the boys away to get ready for riding.

' What will we do with the horses and ponies?' asked Neil.

' They'll all come to Sutherland too,' Alastair assured him, and the boys went away happy, knowing that Alastair would deal with everything for them.

' You know they will always be my responsibility, Cristina?'

' Yes. You could even adopt them. I've always envied people with families.'

His eyes lit up and he gave her the beautifully intimate smile she could never resist.

' Come into the study,' he said, ' and tell me what happened when you spoke to Vernon. And we can make plans.'

She did not want to tell him what Vernon had said. It was all too new and painful.

' Only I'm free,' she said.

' We both are,' he said. ' Free to bind ourselves again in everlasting bondage.'

' Not bondage. In everlasting harmony.'

' Yes,' he said, and took her into his arms and folded her close as if he would never again let her go ; never more to feel : Just this once ; but : For ever and for ever and for ever.

At last, however, they both came down to earth again to make plans.

' You'll like Sutherland, Cristina, I'm sure you will. It's wild and desolate and lonely and I love it like that ; but our own grounds are lovely and the house is ancient and beautiful. I look forward to showing it to you. And my mother is looking forward to retiring into the west wing—well, that sounds rather grand, let's say to her own quarters. She thought it would be for Sylvana to take her place. Now it will be you. She will approve the change, darling: I'm sure she will see you as a far more suitable wife for me and daughter-in-law for her than poor dear Sylvana.'

Cristina smiled, reached up to kiss him lightly on the lips, and said:

'Suddenly I'm acquiring a whole new family. A husband, a mother-in-law, and two sons-more-or-less. And what I suspect is a very grand house.'

'I could hardly take you from a chateau into anything less desirable.' She was still in his arms, and he was gently rubbing her hair with his chin.

Cristina laughed.

'You saw the doll's house I had in London,' she reminded him.

'You're still the lady of the chateau here.'

'I never felt like it. I no longer feel attached to it, and shall happily exchange it for your house, if only because that's where your heart is. But one thing it did, this Chateau de la Falaise, and for that I shall always have a soft spot for it and be grateful to it. It brought us together, Alastair.'

'You might almost say that I'm a part of your legacy,' he said, smiling down at her.

'What a splendid legacy,' she answered, smiling back.

A Treasury of Harlequin Romances!

Golden Harlequin Library

Many of the all time favorite Harlequin Romance Novels have not been available, until now, since the original printing. But now they are yours in an exquisitely bound, rich gold hardcover with royal blue imprint. Three complete unabridged novels in each volume. And the cost is so very low you'll be amazed!

Start your collection now. See reverse of this page for brief story outlines of the FIRST SIX volumes.

Golden Harlequin $1.95 per vol.

Each Volume Contains 3 Complete Harlequin Romances

☐ ## Volume 1

☐ ## Volume 2

Golden Harlequin $1.95 per vol.

Each Volume Contains 3 Complete Harlequin Romances

☐ Volume 3

☐ Volume 4

Golden Harlequin $1.95 per vol.

Each Volume Contains 3 Complete Harlequin Romances

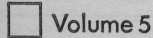 ## Volume 5

LAKE OF SHADOWS by Jane Arbor   887

Kate had to give up her job in London and return to her Irish lakeside home to care for an ailing father — so the man she hoped to marry walked out on her.

MOON OVER THE ALPS by Essie Summers   862

Because of a disappointment in romance, Penny tried to make a new life in a remote sheep station in the New Zealand Alps. Unfortunately it was the one place where this task would prove most difficult!

SHIPS SURGEON by Celine Conway   721

When Pat Fenley boarded the liner "Walhara" to take a young patient to Ceylon, she didn't expect to find that the patient would be in grave danger.

Volume 6

A LONG WAY FROM HOME by Jane Fraser   814

From a lonely, windswept island in the Hebrides to a luxurious villa in the Mediterranean. For Kate Kelsey this meant the prospect of a life of luxury. But what about Jamie?

NEVER TO LOVE by Anne Weale   644

Andrea, a successful model determined to marry Justin for money and security. But once free from financial worries, she began to realise what it was like to live without love.

THE GOLDEN ROSE by Kathryn Blair   650

Once in Mozambique, Gwen finds herself opposing the autocratic Duque de Condeiro whilst helping her uncle and his small motherless son.